"Let's Bury the Past,"

he said softly.

A need, a desperate yearning that had been submerged for so many months now came raging through Jana like a dangerous fever. Her entire body quivered with aching longing. Miles's hand slid up from her waist to caress her through the silky fabric of her dress and she was unaware of a tiny, betraying moan of desire that escaped from her throat.

"I want you, Jana," Miles whispered.

SONDRA STANFORD

fell in love with the written word as soon as she could read one, at the age of six. However, besides her writing ability, she is also a gifted painter, and it was a "struggle to decide which talent would dominate." Fortunately for all her Silhouette readers, the written word triumphed!

Dear Reader:

Silhouette Romances is an exciting new publishing venture. We will be presenting the very finest writers of contemporary romantic fiction as well as outstanding new talent in this field. It is our hope that our stories, our heroes and our heroines will give you, the reader, all you want from romantic fiction.

Also, *you* play an important part in our future plans for Silhouette Romances. We welcome any suggestions or comments on our books and I invite you to write to us at the address below.

So, enjoy this book and all the wonderful romances from Silhouette. They're for *you!*

Karen Solem
Editor-in-Chief
Silhouette Books
P.O. Box 769
New York, N.Y. 10019

SONDRA STANFORD
Tarnished Vows

Silhouette Romance

Published by Silhouette Books New York

America's Publisher of Contemporary Romance

To Huey with Love

SILHOUETTE BOOKS, a Simon & Schuster Division of
GULF & WESTERN CORPORATION
1230 Avenue of the Americas, New York, N.Y. 10020

Copyright © 1982 by Sondra Stanford

Distributed by Pocket Books

ISBN: 0-671-57131-1

First Silhouette Books printing February, 1982

10 9 8 7 6 5 4 3 2 1

America's Publisher of Contemporary Romance

Printed in the U.S.A.

Other Silhouette Books by Sondra Stanford

Golden Tide
Shadow of Love
Storm's End
No Trespassing
Long Winter's Night
And Then Came Dawn
Yesterday's Shadow
Whisper Wind

Chapter One

"You're *what?*" Allen Montgomery exploded. His face, ruddy enough normally, took on a deeper red as he thrust himself from his cushioned chair behind the polished desk and glowered at the girl who stood before him.

"You heard me," Jana Parrish said in a voice that was misleadingly calm. Unconsciously, she stood a little straighter, thrusting her shoulders back. Slender as a reed, dressed in a brown-and-beige plaid skirt, a deep brown blouse, and a beige corduroy blazer, she was the epitome of the smartly attired businesswoman. But the expression on her employer's face was far from businesslike, just as she had known it would be before she had braced herself to speak to him. "I am offering my resignation, effective at five o'clock this afternoon. I'm sorry I can't give you two weeks' notice, Allen, but it's just not possible."

Allen Montgomery was a medium-built man in his

early thirties, and though no one would accuse him of being handsome, he was attractive. In total confusion, he ran a hand across his brow, smoothed back his already smooth brown hair, and swiftly walked around the desk until he was standing only inches from Jana. He grasped her shoulders tightly. "Has someone made you angry?" he demanded. "Has one of the men in the office made a pass at you? If so, tell me!"

Jana shook her head, and her long, silky brown hair swished against her collar. The winter light that fell across the room from the window played over the crown of her head and gave an iridescent glow to her face. "It's nothing like that at all." For the first time, her voice shook. She thrust a piece of paper toward him. "It's a letter from Dorothy Parrish," she told him. "She needs me."

Allen's hazel eyes were puzzled as he looked at her, as though if he stared long enough, intently enough, he would be able to read her mind. But after a moment, in a slow, reluctant movement, he took the letter from her.

"I don't understand," he said when he had finished reading it. "She says she needs you urgently and wants you to come at once, without delay. But why, Jana? You can't just rush off because one old woman sends you a vague message like this."

Jana's soft, pink lips curved into a tiny smile. "You wouldn't call Dorothy old if you knew her," she stated firmly. "But to answer your question, I don't know why she needs me. I only know she wouldn't ask me unless it was important."

"So you're going." Allen's voice was flat.

Jana nodded and briefly caught her lower lip between her teeth. "Dorothy was very good to me at a time in my life when I desperately needed help.

This is the first time she's ever asked anything of me. I have no choice but to go."

Allen glanced at the letter again. "How did she get your address? I thought you told me the Parrishes didn't know where you were."

"Except for Caroline. At Christmas I sent a gift for Dorothy to Caroline's apartment with a note telling her where I was but asking her to keep it a secret from the rest of the family."

"Much good it did," Allen grumbled.

"Caroline wouldn't have betrayed my confidence without a good reason," Jana said with conviction. "Despite everything else, she's still the best friend I have in the world."

Allen dropped the letter, and with a forlorn flutter it landed on his desk. "You can't go, Jana. I'll bet it's a trick of some sort. Besides, what about us?"

"There is no us, Allen, and you know it," Jana said softly.

"I'm in love with you and I want to marry you!" His rising temper made his voice explosive again. "How can you say there's no us?"

"I'm already married," she reminded him gently.

"Well, there's no good reason to be," Allen said curtly. "You haven't seen the man in six months or better. For all you know, *he* may have already divorced *you!*"

"Caroline would have told me if he had," Jana stated positively. "Besides, the Parrish pride has never allowed for divorce."

"That's the most ridiculous thing I ever heard of in this day and age!" Allen said derisively. "Is that what's kept you from starting proceedings yourself?"

"Partly," she admitted with frank honesty. Her gray eyes clouded thoughtfully. "Not for myself or out of any consideration for Miles, but because I know it would hurt Dorothy."

"You're allowing that woman far too much influence over your life," Allen fumed, "letting her feelings hold you bound in a senseless marriage, and now here you are, ready to drop everything and go running back the minute she beckons. Call her." He waved a hand in the direction of the telephone on the desk. "Call her now and find out what this emergency is all about. Maybe you can sort it out over the phone instead of rushing off to Charleston."

"No, I've made up my mind, Allen. I'm going back. No matter why Dorothy needs me, it's time for me to face up to things anyway. I should see Miles again and get our lives straightened out somehow."

Allen frowned. "Will you be coming back?"

"I don't know. I really don't." Jana sighed and lowered her eyes from his face, unable to bear the look of hurt that was plain to see.

"I'll hold your job open until I hear from you," Allen said.

"No, don't do that," she said quickly. She lifted her gaze to his face again and added insistently, "I don't have any idea how long I'll be there or what I'll want to do afterward. And if Miles makes trouble about a divorce, there would be no use in my coming back anyway."

"There would still be your job, for as long as you wanted it, Jana!" Allen said in a pleading voice.

She smiled and gently touched his arm. "I know that," she agreed softly, "but it would be hard on both of us, just as it already is. It's better to end it now before either of us gets hurt."

Allen's lips twisted into a bitter smile. "Meaning I'm not hurt right now?"

"I hope not." Her words were husky, and she had

to clear her throat before going on. "I care a great deal about you as a friend. I hope you'll find the right woman to marry, someone who has a whole heart to give you. But that girl," she ended sadly, "isn't me."

"It's still your husband, then?" he asked in a low voice.

"I'm not sure exactly how I feel about Miles anymore," Jana answered, "but I do know I haven't forgotten him."

Allen stepped back. "Then there's nothing left for me to say except best wishes and I hope life treats you well."

"Thank you," Jana said shakily. "I wish you the same." She bridged the small space between them, stood on her tiptoes, and kissed his cheek.

That evening her roommate, Holly Wilson, watched glumly while Jana packed, and she was no more in favor of the move Jana was about to make than Allen Montgomery had been.

"This is the silliest thing I ever heard of," she said as she perched on one edge of the bed while Jana loaded clothes into her suitcase on the opposite side. "Throwing away a fantastically good job just on Dorothy Parrish's whim, when you don't even know why she wants you. You're not secretly planning to go back to that husband of yours, are you?"

Jana laughed and shook her head. "Not a chance," she said firmly. "I intend to see him, of course, and discuss the possibility of a divorce. But I'm going strictly because of Dorothy. You know how much she's done for me through the years, Holly. I *have* to go."

There was little about Jana that Holly didn't know. Next to Caroline Parrish, Holly was Jana's dearest friend. They had been roommates all through their years at the University of South Carolina in Columbia, and Holly was well aware that Dorothy Parrish had paid for Jana's education.

"I suppose you do, at that," she grudgingly agreed at last. "But I'm going to miss you."

Jana smiled. "I'll miss you, too. And I appreciate your letting me live with you these past few months."

"Well, what are friends for?" Holly asked with exasperation. Her keen brown eyes darkened. "Your room will still be waiting if you want to come back."

"Thanks," Jana responded. "I may take you up on that."

Early the following morning Jana set out in her small Dodge. A gloomy winter gray shrouded Atlanta's skyline as she headed east, and the warmth that emanated from the heater inside the car was welcome.

There had been a tearful parting from Holly, and Jana's thoughts dwelled affectionately on her friend as she reached the edge of the city. Six months ago she had come here, broken and filled with heartache, and had headed like a homing pigeon to Holly's apartment. Leaving Miles as precipitately as she had, she had not known where else to go except to join her old college friend, who had moved directly to Atlanta after graduation, while Jana had gone instead to Charleston to be married. Holly had welcomed her with good-hearted generosity and had insisted upon Jana's moving in permanently with her. Holly was a newspaper reporter, an excellent one, hard-nosed and persistent in ferreting out news. But she had asked no questions of Jana and had waited patiently until Jana was ready to discuss her disastrous marriage.

During her months in Atlanta, Jana had slowly rebuilt her life and her shattered self-esteem. Almost immediately she had landed a job with Allen as personnel director for his supermarket chain, and gradually their business relationship had turned into friendship and might have become something more if Jana had permitted it. Now she told herself bitterly that she was probably being the biggest fool in the world. Allen had made no secret of his love for her and his desire to marry her. If she had any sense at all, she would turn back now, call Dorothy and say she could not come, file for a divorce, and make plans to marry Allen. He, too, had an unhappy marriage behind him, yet to her he was consistently kind and generous, and she was certain they could have a happy marriage together.

There was only one problem with that idea. Jana, though extremely fond of Allen, knew she was not in love with him. His love was not the kind she had known in the past.

Ever since she had received Dorothy's letter, she had rigidly kept all thoughts of Miles at bay. But now, alone with nothing to distract her, memories came flooding back. Visions of Miles smiling tenderly at her, his chiseled lips softened in passion, returned to taunt her. Her treacherous heart leaped as she recalled the nights she had spent in his arms, lacing her fingers through his midnight-black hair or roaming her hands over his broad chest and silky back as he made love to her. Her body heated and ached with unfulfilled desire just at the thought. For months she had carefully blocked out such memories, but today the dam seemed to have burst. And close behind the pictures of their lovemaking came the vision of the last time she had seen him. Once again, an agonizing pain stabbed through her.

It was inevitable that she would see him now that she was going back, and the pertinent question was, what kind of fool was she being by returning to invite

yet more pain? Instinct told her that whatever lay
ahead, whatever Dorothy needed her for, would be
paid for at a dear cost to herself. Doubts and anxiety
over the wisdom of what she was doing nagged at
her, and with every mile Jana grew more nervous
while her stomach knotted with dread.

It was early afternoon when she approached
Charleston. Familiar moss-draped trees came into
sight, and Jana felt she could almost smell the ocean,
even though her car windows were closed against the
dreary day.

A fine, misting rain was falling, reinforcing her
melancholy mood, when she entered the city. She
slowed her speed, unconsciously reluctant to reach
her destination. But at length she got off the express-
way and turned onto Meeting Street, heading toward the old section of the city.

When she reached East Battery, tall palmettos
drooped dolefully in the rain, and far out in the
harbor Fort Sumter, where the first shots of the Civil
War had been fired, was completely obscured by the
leaden sheet of rain. This nasty February day was a
far cry from last summer when Jana had so enjoyed
strolling down the historical cobblestone streets,
appreciating the quaint beauty of old houses and
wrought-iron fences that were characteristic of
Charleston.

She turned off the street, going through the
opened wrought-iron gates that fronted the stately
old, white, three-storied house. Majestic piazzas
where gracious ladies and gentlemen of the past had
enjoyed a cool summer's breeze extended out from
the house on each floor level. The house had been
built by the first Miles Parrish in 1814 with the
fortune he had acquired from rice. Unlike so many
of the grand old houses of Charleston, this one had
never left the hands of its original family, and

someday the present Miles Parrish would be the possessor of it.

Today Jana paid scant attention to the house, or to the gardens that in another month or two would be brilliantly colored with camellias, azaleas, and white magnolia blossoms with their sweet perfume. She parked the car in the drive, braced herself for the raw, wet weather, opened her door, and made a dash for the steps.

It had never been a policy in the Parrish family to stand on ceremony when they visited each other's homes. If the door was unlocked, one simply opened it and walked inside. Jana did so now, quickly, in a hurry to get out of the bone-chilling elements.

The spacious entry hall was exactly as it had been the last time she had seen it. A winding staircase rose to the second floor from the back of the hall. The hardwood floors were polished to such a sheen that she could see her reflection at her feet. A few steps beyond her was a dusky rose-colored Aubusson carpet. A dried plant arrangement was placed on the center of a marble-topped table standing against one wall with a gold-leafed mirror hung above it.

Jana slipped out of her coat, hung it on the coat tree near the door, and then went toward the mirror, attempting to smooth her mist-beaded hair into place.

"Jana!" a familiar voice suddenly squealed. "When did you arrive? I thought you'd call first to let us know when to expect you!"

Jana turned toward the voice and watched as her old friend descended the stairs. Caroline had never looked more beautiful, she thought fleetingly as the other girl came toward her. She was casually dressed in gray wool slacks and a thick white sweater, and her black hair was braided and pinned close to her head. On anyone else, the style would have been

severe; on Caroline it was magnificent, for it emphasized the classic bone structure of her face. Soft
black eyebrows winged above sparkling blue eyes,
and her lips were parted in a smile, revealing even
white teeth.

"It's so wonderful to see you!" she exclaimed as
she warmly embraced Jana. Then, anxiously: "I
hope you're not angry with me for giving Mom your
address. She knew I had it after you sent that
Christmas gift, and she practically nagged me to
death until I told her. *You* know how Mom can be!"

"Why does she want to see me, Caroline?" Jana
asked as they turned toward the living room.

Caroline shrugged her shoulders lightly, but there
was a sudden wariness in her eyes. "I'd rather let her
tell you," she said frankly. "Right now she's taking a
nap, but she'll be down soon, I imagine. Would you
like a cup of hot tea, Jana?"

"I'd love it," Jana answered gratefully, trying to
conceal the chattering of her teeth.

"Be right back, then. Go on in and sit down."

Jana entered the charming living room alone.
While the inherent beauty of the room had been
maintained with rose damask swag draperies and
luxurious patterned carpeting, concessions to mod-
ern comfort had been made as well, and cushioned
sofas and chairs were grouped near the ornate
fireplace. A glittering crystal chandelier hung from
the ceiling in the center of the room.

It was a room that offered memories of happier
days to Jana. She had spent a number of Christmases
here when she and Caroline had been teenagers. It
was here that Miles had first really noticed her, had
realized she had become a woman. And it had been
here that he had presented her with her engagement
ring, a large, brilliant diamond that now rested in its
original box along with the plain gold wedding band.

She shook her head, as though to be rid of the memories. This was now, today, and she had not returned here of her own accord. It was best to bury a past that, while joyful then, could only bring pain to the present.

Caroline returned, bearing a silver tray that held two cups of steaming tea. As Jana reached for her cup she caught a glimpse of another diamond ring, this one on Caroline's left hand.

"You're engaged!" she gasped in shock.

Caroline grinned impishly, the way she had been wont to do in their school days. "I was wondering how long it would take you to notice." She set the tray down on a table and extended her hand so that Jana could adequately admire the ring.

"It's lovely," Jana said, but the expression on her face was still one of bafflement. "But when . . . and who?"

Caroline gracefully sat down on the sofa beside her. "His name is Bill Kirby," she answered readily, "and we're being married next month."

"Next month!" Jana shrieked. "Why didn't you tell me?" There was reproach and the tiniest shred of hurt in her voice.

Caroline leveled her clear, direct gaze upon Jana. "He gave me the ring at Christmas, but"—she shrugged—"though I wanted to call you, I had a feeling you might not be interested, since I *am* Miles's sister."

"What an idiot you are!" Jana scolded. "Of course I'm interested. Our friendship doesn't have a thing to do with Miles."

"I agree," Caroline said soberly, "but I wasn't sure you'd still feel that way since you left him. What happened, anyway? Even Miles didn't know where you had gone. No one did until you sent that gift for Mom and wrote me that one letter."

"Miles never explained?" Jana asked tensely.

Caroline grimaced. "Now what kind of dumb question is that? Since when did Miles ever explain anything to anybody in his life unless he wanted to do so?"

"I suppose you're right," Jana said slowly. In truth, she would have been astonished to learn that he *had* offered an explanation to his family for her leaving; certainly he wouldn't have given the real reason. She shook her head and forced a smile to her lips. "Let's not talk about that right now," she said quickly. "Tell me about your Bill."

Her friend was happy to oblige. "He's a lawyer like Guy is, so that'll make two of them in the family. He lives in Columbia, and in fact I met him through Miles when he came down to discuss business with him concerning that factory he bought there. He's handsome and wonderful and . . ." She was unable to elaborate further on her fiancé just then because at that moment her mother entered the room.

Dorothy Parrish was an older, more reserved version of her daughter. At sixty, she was still beautiful, with sharp blue eyes and lovely silver hair that was swept back from her face in delicate waves. Her petite figure was as slender as it had been when she had been Caroline's age, and just now she was stylishly dressed in a magenta-colored skirt and blouse that lent her a deceptively young and carefree look.

Jana swiftly got to her feet and went forward to meet her mother-in-law, who fondly embraced her. "I'm so thankful you've come, my dear," Dorothy said fervently. "I appreciate it very much."

"You knew I would," Jana replied. "So, now, what's this all about?"

Dorothy Parrish sent a meaningful glance to her daughter and, as though by prearrangement, Caroline rose to her feet, saying smoothly, "I've got a few things I need to attend to. I'll talk with you later, Jana."

"Are you going back to your apartment now?" Jana asked, intending to invite herself to spend the night there.

"Oh, I gave it up," Caroline replied. "Right after I got engaged. I'm staying here with Mother until the wedding, so I'll be around when you two finish talking."

Once they were left alone, Dorothy, who still held Jana's hand in hers, said quietly, "Let's sit down."

Jana looked at the older woman assessingly as they settled themselves on the sofa Caroline had just vacated. The smile of welcome that had been on Dorothy's face when she first entered the room was gone, and replacing it was a heavy sadness.

"Miles isn't hurt . . . or ill, is he?" Jana asked in sudden alarm. Strangely enough, until this very moment such a possibility had simply not occurred to her, but now the thought sent a tingling chill up her spine.

"No, no," Dorothy said hastily. "He's fine . . . at least physically."

"But there is something wrong with him," Jana said flatly, reading the concern in Dorothy's eyes. She sucked in a deep breath. "You might as well tell me straight out."

Her mother-in-law's lips parted in a tight little hint of a smile. "You always were that way, weren't you, child? Wanting everything on top of the table, cards face up."

"It's the only way to face unpleasantness," Jana stated emphatically, "and whatever you're about to tell me *is* unpleasant, isn't it?"

Unhappiness glazed Dorothy's eyes before she nodded. "I suppose I'd better begin by telling you that there are people in the state who are encouraging Miles to run for Congress in the next election. Perhaps you've already heard about that?"

Dazedly, Jana shook her head. "No," she said in a low voice. "I didn't know. Is he going to do it?"

Dorothy sighed. "I don't know. I want him to, and I know that he wants to do it—*wanted,*" she corrected her tenses. "But whether or not he will remains to be seen. In fact, Jana, I'm afraid it will all depend on you."

"I don't . . ." Jana gave her head a negative shake. "I don't understand what you mean. Miles and I have been separated for over six months. How could anything he wants to do depend on me?"

The hand that still held hers tightened, and the force of its pressure warned Jana that they were now getting to the heart of the matter. "If Miles is to have even a ghost of a chance at Congress, it'll have to be with your help, my dear. I want you to come back to him. I *beg* of you to come back to him at once before he's ruined!" For the first time Dorothy's voice trembled.

"Ruined?" Jana echoed blankly. She was shocked to see tears glazing Dorothy Parrish's eyes.

"It's all Guy's fault," Dorothy said abruptly. "Or, rather, Edie's. Oh, Jana, it's all so awful, so sordid."

A cold sense of fatalism settled over Jana, and she sucked in a breath and waited, bracing herself for the rest.

In a shaking voice Dorothy went on, hurriedly reciting the distasteful facts. "Guy has left Edie and plans to sue her for a divorce on grounds of . . . of . . ." Her voice broke over the ugly word. ". . . adultery."

"And he's naming Miles as corespondent," Jana said in an odd, detached sort of voice.

"How did you know?" Dorothy stared at her in surprise.

Jana shrugged, trying to maintain a calm front for Dorothy's sake. "Why else would Guy's divorce concern Miles . . . or me?"

Dorothy nodded. "Of course. Then I don't need to explain how devastating all this is to us as a family, but also to Miles's chances at winning an election."

"Yes." Jana stared thoughtfully down at her hand, which was still being tightly clasped. "If Guy does this, Miles wouldn't even be able to get elected dogcatcher."

"Exactly," Dorothy replied. "So you can see why it's so important for you to come back to Miles, can't you? To put a stop to this scandal before it gets started. If you're back with him, I'm sure then we'll be able to talk some sense into Guy and get him to drop his plans to file this suit. Or at least not to involve Miles in it."

"What happened to cause Guy to decide to do this?" Jana's voice was cold and as brittle as ice. "You may as well tell me everything, Dorothy."

Dorothy flinched and did not meet Jana's gaze. "Edie told Guy that Miles and she were . . . well, you know . . ." she hedged uncomfortably. "But Miles denies it, and I believe him. He's never lied to me before, and I simply can't imagine him getting involved with his own brother's wife. Miles wouldn't do that."

Oh, wouldn't he? Jana thought bitterly, but she remained silent. Just because she had been hurt badly was no reason to add to the pain Dorothy was already suffering.

But she was silent for so long that at last Dorothy squirmed nervously. "I don't know what happened between you two, my dear," she said hesitantly, "to cause you to leave my son, but I'm pleading with you now to come back to him."

Unable to sit still any longer, Jana got to her feet and went to stand before the fireplace, where logs lay in readiness for an evening fire. She shook her head, unconscious of doing it. "You don't know what you're asking of me," she murmured.

The older woman came to stand beside her. "Yes," Dorothy said earnestly. "I do. I'm asking much, perhaps more than you can give, but I'm still asking it. Jana, it's more than just the public embarrassment if Guy should carry through his plans. It's far more than Miles's possible chance at becoming a senator like his father was. It's our *family* I'm asking you to save! As things are now, Guy and Miles refuse to speak to each other and talk this thing out. Edie is alone out there in that enormous house on Kiawah Island and, according to Caroline, in a constant state of hysterics. And Caroline is torn apart, too, what with all this friction and her wedding next month. And I . . ." she ended simply, "am heartbroken. We need you, Jana. We all need you desperately."

For a long time there was only a tense silence in the room. Every instinct in Jana rebelled at what Dorothy was asking of her, and yet she could neither forget nor ignore the vast debt that she owed to this wonderful lady.

Finally, she lifted her gaze from the darkened grate to Dorothy's face and asked, "What does Miles say to the idea of my returning to him?"

Dorothy had the grace to flush. "He doesn't know. I didn't tell him I was asking you to come."

Jana was stunned. "Not tell him?" she cried. "Dorothy, I can't just walk back into his life as though nothing had happened, without any warning at all!"

"Well, I couldn't tell him you were coming," Dorothy said practically, "because I wasn't sure you would. Or that you'd agree to what I'm asking. But again, Jana, I beg you to do it. I know Miles can be obstinate, but I know, too, that you'll be able to convince him of the necessity of this." Now she added in a softer voice, "I have a shrewd notion that the only reason neither of you has divorced the other is that you both realized how badly it would hurt me. I've always been so staunchly against divorce. But if you'll do this, stay with Miles at least until after next year's election, I'll even help you get your divorce if it's what you want. I'll help you financially if you need it, I'll help you any way I can . . . and you'll have my undying gratitude. Please, Jana, save my family!"

Two hours later, several streets away from the Battery, Jana waited for Miles in the house she had left behind six months ago. Her suitcases were in the spare bedroom. She had unpacked only a copper-toned, long-sleeved velour dress and fresh underwear, which she changed into after a long, hot bath. But though she was finally warm, there was an inner chill now that had her quaking.

But she carefully masked all signs of turmoil when at last she heard Miles's key in the door. She rose from her chair, squared her shoulders, and clasped her hands behind her in a determined effort to steady them.

Miles entered the room, and Jana had a brief span of time to study him before he realized she was there. He was neatly dressed in a charcoal-gray suit that fit him to perfection, though it was now splattered by raindrops. The jacket stretched tautly across his strong shoulders, tapering in at the narrow waist, and the slacks emphasized his long legs and slightly hugged his powerful thighs. His jet-black hair, disarrayed as though he had absent-mindedly run his fingers through it, glistened wetly, and one lock drooped across his forehead.

But it was his profile that arrested Jana's attention —the sharply planed slant of his forehead and cheekbones, his smoothly carved nose, his well-defined mouth that just now looked granite hard, though she knew how full and sensuous the lower lip could be, and the arrogance of that square-shaped jawline, which merged with the jutting chin.

All those features went to make the tall man who had turned to close and lock the door. In that fractional instant of appraisal, Jana was hit full force by his masculine magnetism, and her heart twisted in an ache of regret for things past, things that could never be again.

And then he turned and saw her. Jana's heart stopped and she held her breath awaiting his reaction, which was not long in coming. Miles's dark brown eyes widened in shock, and for a long, frozen moment neither of them moved, neither of them spoke.

Then the dark eyes hardened, revealing not even the smallest hint of the tenderness they had once held whenever he had looked at her. There was no gentleness softening his lips. The cold hostility with which Miles was regarding her vibrated between them like a living entity.

The tension between them was heavy, like the leaden skies outside, and it seemed to go on endlessly. But at last Miles broke it. He tossed his briefcase onto the sofa and then took several menacing steps toward her. His face was darkly colored by suppressed fury when he stopped only scant inches from her.

"My dear, *dear* wife," he said scornfully. "May I ask to what I owe this honor? Let me guess! You've come to ask me for a divorce at long last." His hands knotted and went to his waist, and his lips twisted in unmistakable contempt.

Jana flinched and paled beneath the shock of his disparagement, and then her own anger rose to match his. "I'm sure it would please you if I had, but, on the contrary, I've come back to you."

"And what," he asked in a scathing voice, "makes you think for one second that I will take you back? Do you set such great store by yourself that you believe you can just breeze back in here exactly the way you breezed out and I'll bow down in some sort of gratitude?"

Fire blazed in Jana's eyes as she glared at him. "To tell you the truth, I don't care in the least what *you* think or believe! I came back because Dorothy asked me to. Among other things, she wants to save your precious reputation, such as it is."

"Ah!" Miles tossed his head back, then nodded. "I begin to see the light," he said. "She told you about Guy."

"Correct. I'm to come back and in the eyes of the world be your *loving* wife again until next year after the elections. It should be effective in getting Guy off your back and helping your political ambitions as well. After all, every well-equipped Senate hopeful has a smiling, agreeable wife to back him up." She shrugged her shoulders negligently, but her eyes narrowed with purpose. "And then, after all the other votes are in and counted, I'll vote for a divorce."

"Win or lose, hmm?" Miles asked sarcastically. "But if I win, you just might elect to stick it out, mightn't you?"

"Whether you win or lose, *I'll* be the winner, Miles," she answered. "Because then I'll be through with you for good."

Miles's hands went out to grip her arms, and his fingers dug painfully into her flesh. "You've got it all planned, don't you?" he growled. "And what about me? Don't I have any say in the matter?"

"Actually, no," Jana flung at him. "No more than I do, because I don't believe you want to see your mother hurt, either, by the scandal Guy will create if he carries out his plan. Let go of my arms, please," she added crisply. "I have no desire for you to touch me, now or ever again. Which reminds me—I'll be sleeping in the spare bedroom, of course."

Instead of releasing her, Miles increased the pressure of his fingers on her arms until she murmured in protest. But Miles seemed not to notice in his anger, as his intense gaze burned across her face before sweeping derisively down the front of her body, pausing significantly from time to time at strategic locations.

But then, with startling abruptness, he turned from her in disgust, as though he could no longer bear even the sight of her. Which was strange, really, thought Jana indignantly, considering the circumstances. It should be herself, not Miles, who was experiencing that particular emotion.

"I won't go along with it," he said gruffly. "I'll be damned if I'll hide behind any woman's skirts, particularly yours. I don't need you to protect me from my brother or to help me win an election. The last thing I need is a wife who isn't a wife!"

"And the last thing I need," Jana said coldly, "is an unfaithful husband, but it looks as though we're stuck with each other for the time being. Unless," she added, challenging him, "you want to tell Dorothy yourself that you'd rather bring shame and scandal down upon the family. It is, of course, entirely up to you."

Miles half turned to give her a pained look of exasperation, but, all the same, she read the sudden defeat in his eyes. Defeat like that she had already suffered earlier today.

Wearily, she wondered who would be the winner of this new battle that was to be waged in a city that had already earned itself a place in history for a larger war that had been fought more than a hundred years ago.

Chapter Two

With head bowed, Miles stared broodingly into the cold, empty hearth of the fireplace. Jana watched him silently, wondering at the tumble of emotions that must be jumbling his mind. He couldn't possibly want her back any more than she wanted to be here, and yet his love for his mother gave him no choice.

At last he lifted his head and turned, and though his face was drained of color, a whimsical smile flitted across his lips as he met her questioning gaze.

"I need a drink," he acknowledged. "What about you?"

In spite of herself, Jana smiled in sympathetic response. "You know," she said lightly, "that's the best offer I've had all day. Would you like me to fix them?"

Miles shrugged. "It looks as though you're back to stay whether either of us likes it or not, so you may as well make yourself at home again." He shed his coat and began tugging at his tie as though it were strangling him.

Jana walked across the room to the sideboard where the decanters and glasses were and poured Scotch and water into one glass, vodka and tonic into another. The action was automatic and mechanical, for she had done it almost every evening during their marriage.

Miles was seated when she returned with the drinks. "Almost like the old days, isn't it?" he taunted as he accepted the glass. Their fingers brushed fleetingly during the exchange, and Jana snatched hers away quickly. Even that brief touch between them sent an electrical current flowing through her.

"Almost," she agreed as she sank into a nearby chair. "Except that everything is different beneath the surface." Her emotions were under control again now. She leveled a cool glance at her husband and stated quite calmly, "The difference being that you'll never have the opportunity to hurt me again now that I know you so well."

"You don't know me at all," Miles contradicted in a harsh tone. He swirled the ice around in his glass, moodily staring into it. "You only think you know what you saw. You didn't bother to hang around to hear the truth." There was an accusation in his voice, as though he were blaming her for the break-up of their marriage.

Jana stared at the face of the man she had loved, and she had to steel herself against the attraction of it, against the memory of how it felt to be kissed by those lips, to cup that face between her hands, to thrill to the incredible warmth that could light those eyes. She reminded herself that all that was in the past, and now her smile was bitter. "Actions speak louder than words," she said in a clipped voice. "I can't imagine anything you might have said that would have made your behavior acceptable. And in light of Guy's impending suit, it merely confirms what I saw that day."

"It merely confirms that Edie is a liar and a troublemaker and that Guy is a fool not to realize it," Miles grated. His eyes narrowed with anger as he glared at her. "But I have no intention of trying to change your opinion or make any explanation at this late date."

"That's fine with me," Jana assured him, "because you would only fail. I wouldn't believe a word you said." She took a sip of her drink and leaned back in her chair. "By the way," she said in that same cool, controlled voice, "your mother expects us for dinner tonight."

Miles's lips twisted into a sardonic grin. "She seemed very sure, then, that I would accept you back."

Jana nodded. "I suppose she was. In all the years I've known her, this is the first time I've ever seen her pressure others into doing what she wants. Except," she added with a tiny smile of grim pleasure, "with my stepfather."

Miles gave a humorless laugh. "Oh, Mom is very deceptive. Most of the time she comes across as sweet and agreeable, but she always did have a hand of iron that she used whenever she believed in something strongly enough. She even used it on Dad when she forced him to retire after he had that first neart attack. But by making him give up the heavy pressures of politics, she added years to his life." He polished off his drink, stood up, and said, "Well, if we've got a command appearance tonight, I suppose I'd better go take a shower and change." His dark eyes were mocking as he glanced down at her. "I don't suppose you laid out my clothes for me the way you always used to do?"

Jana shook her head. "I didn't even think of it. I don't consider myself a *wife* anymore, you see."

Miles's dark gaze sizzled as it swept over her slowly and analytically, as though he found something lacking in what he saw. "No," he said, nodding. "Neither do I." Without another word, he left the room.

Jana was left alone with wildly fluctuating emotions. Her gaze darted around the room, touching on the bright gold draperies at the windows, the Queen Anne desk nearby, and the piecrust table that held a lamp. The orante cornice that traveled across the top of the walls framed the fireplace mantel with its French clock in a glass case. What joy she had experienced when she had made each of the furniture and accessory purchases herself after Miles had bought this house! It was not as large or as grand as his mother's, but it was graceful and beautiful, and Jana had loved it. She had visualized it as a warm and wonderful home, a happy place to raise a family.

Fiercely, she clamped a tight lid on that disturbing thought. It was an exercise in futility. There *had* been no family during their year together, and thank heaven for that! At least, when the end had come, there had been no one else to consider except herself, no one else to suffer besides herself.

And yet here she was, back in the house she had never expected to set foot inside again, about to resume at least an outward semblance of a marriage with a man who didn't want her, a man she did not want. It was senseless, and Jana's intuition told her that it would turn out to be a disastrous mistake. But, all the same, she was bound to try because of her love for and her debt to Dorothy.

What a difference there was between the young woman of twenty-three she was today and the frightened teenager she had been when Dorothy Parrish first made such a dramatic impact on her life.

Despite her broken marriage, there was a self-assurance deep within Jana that had been entirely lacking in her as a child. Today she knew herself to be attractive, but, far more important, she had confidence in her ability to run her own life. Dorothy had seen to it that she had been provided with an excellent education, and Jana had no doubts that she could always support herself. She had proved that to her own satisfaction when she had worked as personnel director at Miles's clothing factory after their marriage, as well as with the job she had later held with Allen Montgomery.

Jana's father had died when she had been just a small child, and when she was seven her mother had remarried. Although Jana knew her mother had loved her, she had lacked a certain strength and had been unable or unwilling to interfere with her second husband's treatment of her child.

Even now, so many years later, Jana's shoulders tensed, her entire body went rigid, at the thought of Harv Curtis. No matter how hard she had tried to please him, it had been impossible. Whatever chore he might set her to do, she could never quite do it right. No matter how excellent her grades were at school, they were never good enough. He had told her repeatedly how plain she looked, how stupid she was, how lazy she was, and Jana cringed at the memory of him shouting at her, forcing her to go without supper as punishment for some minor infraction of a rule.

Jana shivered, took another sip of her drink, then stood up and went across to the window, where she gazed unseeingly at the rain splattering against the windowpanes.

Dorothy Parrish and Jana's mother had been girlhood friends growing up in Charlotte, North Carolina. Though they had only rarely seen one another after they were married, they had kept in touch.

Her mother had died in a car accident when Jana was fourteen, and that was when Dorothy swooped down upon them and forever changed her life. A neighbor had helped them out by going through the family's address book, telephoning friends to tell them of the tragic death of Ann Curtis, and Dorothy had flown in for the funeral. She had taken an immediate liking to Jana, and her sharp eyes had not missed the hostile way Harv Curtis treated the young girl. She had bluntly asked if he wanted to continue raising Jana or whether he would like to be free of the responsibility, since she was not his natural child and he had never legally adopted her. He chose freedom, and almost before she realized it Jana had become Dorothy Parrish's legal ward, had been outfitted with the most wonderful new wardrobe, and had been packed off to the same exclusive boarding school Caroline attended.

The two girls had become instant and firm friends, as their mothers had been. To all intents and purposes, Jana had become an official member of the Parrish family.

"You look as though your mind is a thousand miles away," a deep voice said from behind her.

Jana turned from the window to see Miles standing close behind her. He had changed into a dark blue suit, and he smelled faintly of aftershave lotion. The scent tugged at her senses, for it was the brand she had always bought for him. Just now his face was sober, his eyes dark and serious.

Jana lightly shrugged her shoulders. "I was about nine years away," she answered. "To the time your mother took me away from Harv Curtis."

Miles frowned and, incredibly, his face softened, for he alone of all the people in the world knew the true story of Jana's unhappy childhood. Though Dorothy had rescued her from it and knew bits and pieces of her background, Miles alone knew all the ugly details. There had been many nights in bed when he had held Jana in his arms and persuaded her to talk about it—"exorcising the evil ghosts," he had called it. Now he said gently, "Don't torture yourself, precious heart. The monster doesn't deserve a moment of time in your thoughts."

Jana gave a shaky laugh. She knew that Miles's pet endearment for her had merely slipped out accidentally from long habit, but, all the same, it shook her. "Thanks," she said, trying to pretend she had not noticed. "Maybe Harv doesn't, but your mother does."

"You really love Mom, don't you?" Miles asked gravely.

"More than that," she replied. "I adore her. There's nothing I wouldn't do for her."

"Including returning to a husband you no longer love." His voice went hard, like flinty steel. The gentleness of a moment ago had evaporated.

Nodding, Jana silently agreed.

"It isn't going to work," he told her. "Mom is wrong. I doubt it'll have any influence on Guy at all, as hotheaded as he is right now, and though your presence would certainly help in the Senate race, *I'm* not asking for your help."

Jana shrugged. "As I said earlier, if you want me to leave now, you'll have to tell Dorothy it's your decision, not mine. This is the only thing she's ever asked of me, and, distasteful though it is, I'll go through with it for her sake. Parrish dignity means a lot to her."

"Don't I know it!" Miles exclaimed hotly. With sudden anger, he pounded a clenched fist into the palm of his other hand. "I could kill Guy for upsetting Mom this way!" he said with impotent fury.

Jana's eyes were cold as she gave him an assessing look. "I imagine Guy could kill you for what you've done. No man relishes his wife having an affair—with his own brother, yet!"

Miles's dark eyes narrowed and his nostrils flared. "I told you it was all a lie!"

Jana laughed, and it was a ragged, unpleasant sound. "And I told *you* I don't believe you. Now we'd better go, or we'll be late for dinner."

It was a miserable meal, not at all conducive to pleasant relaxation, for Dorothy had sprung an unwelcome surprise upon them all. Guy had also been commanded to appear, and now both brothers, neither of whom had expected to see the other, sat glowering across the table at each other.

Somehow they all worked through the meal of pork roast and rice, though the only conversation was between Dorothy, Caroline, and Jana. When the meal drew to an end at last, Dorothy spoke decisively. "We'll all go into the living room now and have a little chat." Though her voice was sweet, Jana detected the hint of iron that Miles had referred to earlier.

They settled themselves like enemies in a war camp around a negotiating table. Miles lowered himself into a chair as far distant as possible from his brother, while Jana, Caroline, and Dorothy took the large sofa. A heavy silence weighted the air.

"You're probably wondering," Dorothy addressed her younger son, "why Jana is here."

Guy gave a slight nod with his dark head. Two years younger than his brother, Guy Parrish was very like Miles in looks. He, too, had thick black hair and dark brown eyes, though he was not quite as tall as Miles, nor was his build quite so impressive. Now his brooding gaze went to Jana. "The question had crossed my mind," he said.

"Jana has returned to Miles," Dorothy stated flatly, "in order to block the plans you have for shaming this family."

Guy leaned forward in his chair. "You think Jana's presence is going to stop me?" he challenged.

Dorothy nodded. "I think so. If Miles's wife is here standing staunchly behind him, you will look like a fool if you go ahead with this outrageous suit."

"It's Miles who will look like a fool," Guy growled. "I'm not dropping it, Mom. On Monday I intend to file, just as I said." He snapped his fingers. "And that," he added, "will be the end of my brother's grand plans for Congress."

"No, Guy," his mother disagreed quietly. "Miles will still run, with Jana's support. And the embarrassment of the suit will be upon you, not him, when people see her standing firmly beside him. But there's something else I must tell you." Her lips quivered, revealing the stress she was under. "If you do this thing, I shall cut you from my will."

Guy stared at her, astounded, and blood slowly coursed into his face. "You don't mean that!"

Dorothy's gaze was unflinching. "I do indeed," she replied. "I will leave your share of my money to Miles."

"*How* can you take his side in this?" Guy cried, jumping to his feet and staring down at his mother in agitation. "Mom, he's wrecked my marriage! He took my wife from me and . . ."

Dorothy held up a hand to silence him. "I know

nothing about the matter," she said. "Only what Edie told you and that Miles denies it. Two very different stories. I'm not a judge, nor do I care to be. The truth doesn't concern me, but my family's reputation in this city does . . . very much! I will not have our name dragged in the mud and be publicly humiliated, Guy! Jana is here to lend credibility to Miles's story in case you go through with this. But I also mean what I said. I will disinherit you and I will no longer claim you as my son if you dishonor your father's fine name!"

Guy threw his hands up with the air of a man being pushed beyond his limits. Suddenly, he whirled to face Jana. "How can you come back and support Miles?" he demanded. "You obviously had good reason to leave him before, so why come back now and do this? You can't love him so much as all that!"

"I came because I care about your mother, which is more," Jana said in a scorching voice, "than you seem to do!"

Guy glared at her, as though by sheer willpower he could draw her over to his side of the quarrel. But as Jana continued to meet his eyes without wavering, it was he who turned away.

"All right," he said at last, facing his mother again. "I'll leave Miles's name out of it if it means that much to you. But I'm going ahead with the divorce, no matter what you say." He turned abruptly and strode toward the door.

Miles jumped to his feet and followed. "Guy, wait!" he ordered in a stern, implacable voice. "I want to talk to you. You *must* listen to me!"

Guy had reached the door, where he paused. "I don't want to hear anything you have to say!"

There was a long, pregnant silence in the room after the shattering slam of the front door. Then

Caroline gave a sad little laugh. "Well," she said, "what a happy family we are!"

And only for Caroline did the remainder of the evening contain any happiness as far as Jana could see. Unless you counted Bill Kirby, of course. For, not fifteen minutes after Guy had stormed out, Caroline's fiancé arrived unexpectedly, delighting his future bride.

Bill was a pleasant-looking young man of medium height and build, with sandy brown hair and calm gray eyes. His handshake was firm and his smile friendly as he was introduced to Jana.

"It's a pleasure to meet you," he said. "Caroline's told me so much about you. I do hope you'll be at our wedding."

Jana returned the smile. "I wouldn't miss it for the world," she told him. "In fact, I doubt it would even be legal if I weren't there to witness it!"

"In that case, you'll have a place of honor," Bill said with a chuckle, "because I certainly want to tie this girl up legally." His arm went around Caroline's waist and he drew her close. "I intend to keep her at my side for the rest of her life."

Caroline gave him an adoring look. "That won't be difficult to do," she said softly, "since it's what I want, too."

Jana happened to glance beyond Caroline to see Miles's sardonic gaze upon them. Was he, she wondered, thinking, as she was, just how quickly those vows of eternal love could be forgotten?

They left shortly afterward, and Jana's thoughts were glum as the Chrysler twisted its way through the narrow streets toward their own house. Beside her Miles was grim and forbidding, his jaw sharply etched against the darkness by passing lights. What, she asked herself, have I gotten myself into by coming back? More important, she wondered if it was possible to actually go through with it, living in an uneasy truce with a husband who didn't want her.

When they reached the house, Miles did not attempt to stop her when Jana headed straight for the spare bedroom, and she was weakly grateful that for this day, at least, there would be no more scenes.

But, exhausted as she was after the long drive from Atlanta and the emotional battle she had fought since arriving in Charleston, sleep eluded her. She had never expected to be inside this house again, and her senses were acutely aware of Miles, sleeping in the next room, *their* room, where her joy had known no bounds whenever he had made love to her. Unbidden memories of their love nights together in the huge bed rose up to torment and mock her. For her it had been so wonderful, next to her idea of heaven. But for Miles, apparently, it had not been enough.

Cold chills assailed her as the ugly memory she had so long blocked out of her conscious thoughts returned. With it, a tight knot formed in her midsection. Everything about that scene came back with stark, appalling clarity. She could even picture the humorous get-well card she had bought standing prominently on the bedside table.

Miles had come down with a virus the week before that dreadful day. He had fought it for a couple of days, continuing to go to the office as usual, fighting chills and fever. But when his cough became severe and the other symptoms did not abate despite all the aspirins he had swallowed, Jana had finally put her foot down, hauled him to the doctor, and then made him go to bed and stay there.

It was the first time he had been ill since their marriage, and he had been a horrible patient, always grumbling and sour. Jana had done her best to make

him comfortable and to cheer him up, bringing him
magazines and books and the get-well card. At the
time they had a part-time maid who came in twice a
week to cook and clean, but Jana had talked the
woman into coming every day for a week. This
ensured that there was someone home to care for
Miles and to see that he had hot meals and took his
medicine while she was at the office. But finally,
after a week in bed, he was definitely on the mend,
though still weak. At Miles's insistence that he was
well enough to take care of himself, Jana had
allowed the maid to take the day off.

Edie, the woman who was even now still affecting
all their lives, seemed always to have been around. It
had never been a secret that she had once been
engaged to Miles, long ago, before Miles had ever
noticed Jana. It had happened while Jana and Caroline had still been in high school, but for some
reason Edie had soon broken the engagement and
then had surprised everybody by marrying Guy. But
whatever the cause of their breakup, apparently it
had not ended the feelings that existed between Edie
and Miles. Otherwise there would not be this problem today, the one that had brought her back to
Charleston. Nor would there have been that scene
months ago that had sent Jana running to hide like a
wounded squirrel.

Jana was helpless to stop her mind from returning
to the past. She had come home from the office early
that day, deciding to surprise Miles by spending a
quiet, pleasant afternoon with him and then later
preparing a tempting meal that she hoped would whet
his appetite. Jana had always rather enjoyed the
evenings when the maid wasn't there and she could
cook a meal herself.

She did not see Edie's car parked in front of the

house, because she had driven in from the back straight into the garage and had let herself into the house quietly through the kitchen door. Then she had gone softly upstairs to the bedroom to check on Miles, keeping quiet in case he was sleeping. But what confronted her eyes was so shocking that she had stood paralyzed in the opened doorway.

Would she never be able to banish that scene from her mind? she wondered dismally as she opened her eyes and stared into the heavy darkness of the bedroom. But even with eyes wide open, she still saw it all. . . . Miles, wearing only his pajama bottoms, sitting on the edge of the bed; Edie in his arms, fervently kissing him, her arms entwined around his neck, one hand caressing his head. The mussed-up bed told its own tale.

Apparently she had made some small noise, giving away her presence, because suddenly the couple had drawn slightly apart and glanced toward her. Edie had merely looked blank; Miles had looked thoroughly shocked, and the horror on his face had galvanized Jana into action. She had whirled about and fled down the stairs and out of the house, totally ignoring Miles's commanding shouts for her to stay. Not knowing where to go, she had finally gone to a motel for the night. The next day she had called Caroline and asked her to go to the house and pack her bags and bring them to her.

God bless Caroline, she thought now. In spite of being Miles's sister, she had come to Jana's aid and had pledged herself to secrecy about where she was going so long as Jana promised to write and send her address. To this day, Caroline had no idea what had brought about the necessity for Jana's leaving; she had not asked questions but had merely pursed her lips together severely and then cursed her brother roundly for having put that wan, devastated look on her friend's face. She had pledged her continuing friendship and further help, if needed.

Thoroughly aroused now by all her disturbing thoughts, Jana knew she would not sleep for hours unless she did something. She had never owned a sleeping pill in her life, so now she flicked on the bedside lamp, crawled out of the bed, and slipped on the apricot negligee that matched her gown. They had been part of her trousseau over a year ago, and because she had been given so many sets by friends for her bridal showers, she had never replaced them with more sturdy, utilitarian night wear.

She padded silently down the dark stairway, knowing her way through the house by touch. At the foot of the stairs she did not even bother flipping on a light in the entrance hall but went swiftly across the black area into the kitchen. Only then did she turn on a light.

The kitchen, like the rest of the house, was unaltered. She found a saucepan; the cocoa and the sugar were exactly where she had always kept them. Now she mixed a container of milk with the other ingredients and placed the pan on the stove.

When the hot chocolate was ready, she poured it into a large mug and went into the living room. She flipped on a lamp and then sat down on the sofa, curling her legs up beneath her.

The hot drink and the stillness of the pleasant room where she had always felt so comfortable combined to soothe her. Jana gradually felt the stiffness release its hold upon her muscles. Her body relaxed, her shoulders lost their tenseness, and the headache that had pounded against her temples began to fade.

Her eyelashes fluttered downward and a wonderful lethargy crept over her, so that she was in a near-somnolent state when Miles found her there. "It's late," he said quietly. "Why are you still up?"

Jana focused her fatigue-glazed eyes upon him, only barely taking in his half-naked state. He wore blue pajama pants but no shirt, and the pale lamplight gleamed against his bronzed chest.

"I couldn't sleep," she murmured fuzzily.

Miles's firm lips softened as he smiled and removed the cup from her limp fingers. "Well, you're almost asleep now, so the cocoa must have done the trick. Come, it's time you were properly in bed." His strong arms went around her back and beneath her legs, and before she could even gather enough wits about her to protest, he was holding her securely against his bare chest and striding toward the stairs.

Upstairs, he carried her into the guest room she was using. With a gentleness about him she had long forgotten he could have, he laid her down and tucked the covers about her.

"Good night, precious heart," he whispered as her heavy eyelids fluttered down to close over her eyes.

"G'night, Miles," she murmured. And almost immediately she fell into a sound sleep.

The next morning Jana awoke sharply. On sight of the room, her awareness of the previous day and why she was here came rushing back like a high tide in the Charleston harbor. Only vaguely was there a recollection of Miles carrying her upstairs and putting her to bed. But, vague or not, she knew it had actually happened. She knew, too, that if she was to get through the next year and a half, she must avoid such intimate situations in the future. It would be all too fatally easy to fall again beneath the spell of Miles's magnetic attraction.

She dressed in black slacks and a black sweater, unrelieved by any jewelery. All she owned these days anyway was the costume variety. When she had left Miles, she had instructed Caroline to leave behind all the jewelry he had given her during their marriage. Now, as she brushed her hair, she wondered grimly whether he still had it or whether he had given it away to Edie. Her sister-in-law would be delighted to have it, secondhand though it might be. Edie had never made any secret of her envy of the things Miles had showered upon Jana, things that Guy had been unable to afford.

How different two brothers could be, Jana thought idly as she sat down on the edge of the bed and slipped on her shoes. Except for now, in his burning anger, Guy had always been the one with the more winning personality. Miles usually had a pleasant and polite way about him toward most people, but there was also a certain measure of reserve about him. Jana knew that few people were ever really close to him or felt they knew him well. After their father's death seven years ago, Miles had taken his share of his inheritance and bought out the clothing factory, a mismanaged and failing concern, and brought it back to its feet by devoting himself to the task night and day. Caroline had invested her share and planned to use it eventually in the future. Only Guy had squandered his share, and Jana suspected that he now regretted his folly; Miles's success must have added to his grievances against his brother, even though Guy was an attorney and most certainly earned an adequate income. But Guy was normally an open and friendly person. He enjoyed being around swarms of people, throwing lavish parties, and taking extravagant vacations. Though Edie might have envied Jana's gifts from Miles, there was no doubt that she had eagerly helped Guy run through the money he had inherited. In the end, they had been reduced to living within his current income from his law practice.

When she left the bedroom, Jana could hear Miles down the hall in the bathroom connected to the master bedroom. Although she could not hear the spray of water, she knew he was in the shower because he was singing cheerfully and off key at the top of his lungs. Almost, the sound brought a smile to her lips; it reminded her of their life together as it had once been. But she remembered in time, caught her lower lip between her teeth, and ran down the stairs.

In the kitchen she put coffee grounds into a paper filter, poured water into the top of the coffee maker, and while it began its chore found sausage and grapefruit in the refrigerator. By the time Miles entered the room, neatly dressed in a gray business suit and a navy-blue-and-silver-striped tie, Jana had pancakes and sausages ready.

"What a nice surprise," Miles said with a slight edge to his voice as he pulled out his chair. "Since you no longer consider yourself a wife, I expected to scrounge for myself the way I've had to do ever since you left."

"I'd let you," she answered acidly, sitting down herself, "if I didn't happen to be hungry, too."

Miles's dark eyebrows came together in a frown. He lifted his cup. "Did you sleep well?" he asked blandly. "Or did you miss the comforts of our own bed?"

"I slept perfectly, thank you," Jana snapped. "And I haven't missed 'our' bed in months, not since I realized another woman had used it!"

The black brows crashed down over snapping dark eyes. "That will be enough of that!" he ordered.

"Oh, will it?" Jana's voice dripped like the maple

syrup she'd been about to pour over her pancakes.
"We're not to speak honestly and openly, is that it?
Is your sense of delicacy offended?"

"Only your barbed tongue is offending me!" Miles
grated. "You never used to be a person who enjoyed
taunting people."

"If I've changed," she said harshly, "it's entirely
thanks to you, and so long as I must live here again, I
have no intention of glossing over anything. You
opened my eyes, Miles Parrish, and taught me to
never again trust any man; taught me, too, to speak
out when something bothers me. And if the truth
bothers *you*, that's your problem, not mine!"

Abruptly, Miles thrust back his chair. He was
around the table in a flash, tightly gripping her upper
arms. He gave her a little shake as she stared at him.
"You little hellcat," he growled. "You're determined to believe what you want to believe. So be it!
I'm damned if I'll ever try to explain anything
different. You say there'll be plain speaking around
here from now on. Well, that suits me fine. For
starters, don't let me catch you running around the
house ever again flaunting yourself in those frilly,
filmy night things of yours like the one you were
wearing last night! Whatever else you may think of
me, I *am* a man. I *am* still your husband, and you
just might find yourself contending with an unwelcome situation!"

He released her and stood glowering at her for an
endless moment; then he turned and walked briskly
from the room.

Chapter Three

Pen in hand, Jana sat at the Queen Anne desk, attempting to write a letter to Holly. Mostly, she stared out the window, her mind drifting from this difficult letter. She had to give her friend some reason why she had returned to Miles, but she did not care to reveal the whole truth. Though Holly had eventually learned the story about Jana's discovering Miles and Edie together, Jana had no intention of telling her now about Edie's claims and all the resulting problems. Holly would think her a complete fool for returning to Miles under such circumstances. Jana thought herself one as well, but there was no reason to let the whole world know, she thought grimly.

At last she withdrew her gaze from the golden sunlight outside and began to write. "Family circumstances are such that I must return to Miles for the present. But I am well and happy, so please don't worry about me." The "happy" part was a complete lie, but she hoped it would satisfy Holly's concern about her.

The truth was that she had never been more unhappy, excepting those miserable years when she had been under Harv Curtis's thumb, or that one shockingly horrible day last year. She had been back now for over a week. Ever since that morning at breakfast when Miles had been so furious with her, they had scarcely exchanged a word. Though they shared the same house, they lived entirely separate lives. Miles came and went as he pleased, and she did the same. They met at the breakfast table and the dinner table and carefully avoided each other the rest of the time.

To make matters worse, Jana was bored. She was used to keeping busy. They had married as soon as she had graduated from the university, and shortly after their honeymoon she had gone to work in Miles's business. After the separation, she had worked for Allen. This was the first time in her life that she was completely at loose ends, with time hanging heavily over her like a shroud of gloom. Even though they only had a part-time maid, she kept the house in such perfect order that there was little for Jana to do except prepare a meal or two on the days Daisy was off.

She was staring into space again, the letter forgotten once more, as she considered the idea of searching for a job. Naturally, her old job at the factory had been filled after she left. Even if it stood open, Jana doubted Miles would want her there again.

The white desk phone suddenly jangled, jolting her out of her reveries. Jana was completely taken aback to hear Miles's voice on the other end of the line.

"Did I catch you at a bad time?" he asked.

"Not at all. To be honest, I'm bored silly," she answered.

Miles chuckled, and it was not an unpleasant sound. "Knowing you, I was wondering how long it would be before you started complaining. We'll have to give it some thought soon."

"Well, thanks," she said, surprised at the understanding tone in his voice.

"Reason I'm calling," he went on now, "is to tell you Sam Nash is in the hospital. He was in a car accident last night and underwent surgery."

"How terrible!" Jana exclaimed. Sam Nash was one of the foremen at the factory, and Jana knew him well from her dealings with him while she had worked there. "Will he be all right?"

"So the hospital told me when I called. But he's pretty banged up, has a broken leg and some internal injuries. However, they say he's conscious and is allowed visitors. I thought I'd drop by to visit him tonight, and I wanted to know whether you'd like to go along."

"Yes," Jana said promptly. "Want me to order some flowers?"

"I already had Kathleen do that," Miles replied, referring to his secretary. "But you might pick up a box of candy or something for us to carry with us."

"All right," she agreed. "I will."

"And, Jana?"

"Yes?"

"Why don't we plan to have dinner out beforehand? Could you go for some seafood?"

For some inexplicable reason Jana's heart flipped over. There was nothing really personal or touching in their conversation, and yet there was that old, familiar friendly note to Miles's voice, the one he had always used only when he spoke to her, a tone of voice that seemed to shut away the rest of the world.

"Love to," she agreed instantly.

"Great!" Somehow, Miles sounded just as glad as she suddenly felt. "I'll see you later, then."

By the time Miles arrived home that evening, Jana was dressed and ready. She was wearing a soft, gold-colored dress with a V neckline and long, tapered sleeves. Her light brown hair had been swept up from her neck and twisted into a sophisticated knot. The dress would have looked better had she worn a bit of jewelry with it, but none of her costume trinkets pleased her. She would, she decided, have to go as she was. Even so, she was not displeased with the results of her hairstyle or of her makeup. The light coating of brown eye shadow gave a mysterious look to her eyes. Her bright orange-red lip gloss gave her face the color it needed so that it would not be overshadowed by the brightness of the dress.

She had Miles's drink mixed and ready for him when he came through the door. He paused as she turned from the sideboard, his glass in her hand. For a long moment they were wordless as they gazed at each other.

Finally, Miles cleared his throat. "You look very beautiful tonight."

Her lips parted in a tiny smile. "Thank you. I . . . I have your drink ready."

She went forward to hand it to him, and for another moment they gazed into each other's eyes as though mesmerized. Standing so close to him, Jana could see his black pupils dilate as he looked at her. She could study every angle of his face, the straight length of his nose, the squared line of his chin, even the tiny network of indentations around his eyes.

"Well," Miles said at last, accepting the drink from her hand, "I guess I'd better shower and change so that we can go."

"Yes, of course." The moment that had held them bound was gone. Quickly, Jana turned back to the sideboard and picked up her own glass.

It's not going to work, she told herself after he went away, and she dropped limply into a chair. *The old feelings are beginning to return.* It was not at all what she had expected.

Strangely enough, when she had first met Miles, she had never dreamed that he would be the man she would someday marry. Those early years after Dorothy had included her as a part of the family, Jana had occasionally seen Miles and Guy, usually during Thanksgiving or Christmas holidays when Caroline and she had been home from school. But whenever they had been around, more often than not they had girlfriends tagging along. And although both young men had treated Jana kindly, they had also treated her as just another younger sister. They had both been well into their twenties at the time, already through with college, while the girls were still struggling through high school.

It had been during Jana's first year in college that she heard from Caroline that Miles was engaged. But it had made little impression upon her, because by then she scarcely ever saw any of the Parrish family. After graduation, Caroline had gone east to Vassar, while Jana had attended the state university in Columbia. Though the two girls still kept in touch by letter or telephone, as they both did occasionally with Dorothy, there were few get-togethers. Once both girls were settled in college, Dorothy began to travel a great deal, flitting from one continent to another the way Jana might go from one side of Columbia to the other.

It was during her senior year at the university that Jana finally saw Miles again. Dorothy was home that Christmas and had insisted that the entire family gather for the holiday, and that had included Jana. By then Guy and Edie had already been married for almost two years. Though Edie and Miles had been constantly thrown together, they had seemed to pay scant attention to each other. Edie had seemed genuinely in love with Guy, while Miles had devoted his attentions exclusively to Jana.

How magical it had all been, she thought now. By the time the new year had rolled around and she had returned for her final semester at the university, they had both known they were in love. Miles burned many a gallon of gasoline driving between Charleston and Columbia to visit her frequently. They had married that June, shortly after her graduation.

"You never touched your drink."

Startled, Jana looked up to see Miles standing beside her chair. He had changed into a pair of dark brown slacks and wore a tan leather jacket with them. He was smiling at her in the friendliest of ways, and his smile snatched at her breath, so that it was a moment before she could trust herself to speak.

She glanced at her drink on the lamp table and shrugged. "I wasn't really in the mood for it." She rose to her feet, saying, "If you're ready to go, I'll just get the candy and book I bought for Sam."

"Just a moment," Miles said. He held out a wooden jewelry box she could not help recognizing as her own. "Your dress," he said critically, "needs a little adornment. Would you wear some of your jewelry . . . and would you also put back on your wedding ring? Please?"

Because it was a request rather than an order, Jana complied. In truth, she had been so upset ever

since her return that she had not even realized she
had never put back on her wedding ring.

"All right." There was a little catch to her voice
that she hoped Miles did not detect. Taking the box
from him, she hurried toward the bedroom.

Five minutes later she rejoined him, wearing a
dainty gold chain necklace with its matching bracelet
and earrings. Her engagement and wedding rings,
which had been stashed away in the depths of one of
her suitcases, flashed on her left hand.

There was an approving light in Miles's eyes when
she returned, but all he said was, "That's better.
Ready to go? I'm starved."

They shared a leisurely dinner at one of Charleston's finest seafood restaurants. For the first time
since her return, the two of them talked easily and
without any hidden undercurrents or sarcasm. Miles
answered her questions about how the factory was
doing, about the new factory he had purchased near
Columbia, about Caroline's fiancé, about friends
they had socialized with during their marriage. He,
in turn, quizzed her about her job in Atlanta and
about her friend Holly, with whom she had lived. In
short, they were catching up on six months' worth of
news. Their questions and answers flowed without
even the shortest awkward pause.

When they were in the car and heading toward the
hospital, Miles cautioned, "By the way, when you
left your job at the factory so abruptly and didn't
return, I let the key employees believe you had fallen
ill. They think that after your recovery you decided
not to go back to work."

Jana smiled wryly. "The Parrish pride again," she
said, but there was no heat to the words.

Miles flashed her an answering smile. "I suppose
you're right," he conceded, "but, anyway, I thought
I'd better let you know before you see Sam."

Sam Nash was a large, burly man with a naturally ruddy complexion, but that evening he bore little resemblance to his normal self. A white bandage was swathed across the top of his head, and his face below it was almost as colorless. His right leg was in a cast and suspended in the air, so that he looked thoroughly uncomfortable. Jana's heart twisted at the sight of such a robust man so totally immobilized.

Standing near his bed when they entered the room was Sam's wife, Diane, whom Jana had met once or twice at company social events.

Despite his condition, Sam's eyes lighted when he saw them. "Hello, boss," he greeted. "Mrs. Parrish, it's nice to see you again. We've missed you at the works."

"How're you doing, Sam?" Miles asked as he approached the bed. "You look like you got tangled up with a cement mixer."

Sam grinned, but the grin was wan. "Feels like it, too," he admitted.

"We brought you a little something, Sam," Jana told him. She placed the box of chocolates on his bedside table and held the book up so that he could view its cover.

"The Old West!" Sam exclaimed with pleasure. "Now, how did you know that was my hobby, Mrs. Parrish?"

Jana laughed. "Because the last time I saw you, you favored me with a brief history lesson about it, that's how."

"Thanks," Sam said with a genuine note of enthusiasm in his voice. "I'll enjoy that. Thanks for the flowers you sent, too."

Now Jana crossed the room, and she and Sam's wife had a soft-voiced conversation near the window while Miles visited with Sam.

They did not stay long; Sam did not look as though he needed prolonged visits. So, after a few minutes, Miles glanced meaningfully at Jana and they bid their good-byes.

There was something different about Miles as they left the hospital. Jana sensed it at once. Gone entirely was his easy, relaxed demeanor from earlier in the evening. Now there was a certain tenseness about him. He was worried about something, and his anxiety communicated itself instantly to her.

As soon as they were inside the car and could speak privately, Jana asked bluntly, "What's the matter? Is Sam injured worse than you had been led to believe?"

Miles shook his head and lit a cigarette. "No, it's not that, though he is pretty banged up and it'll be months before he's back on the job."

"You're concerned about who's going to fill in for him?"

Again Miles shook his head. "No. Young Johnson can do it. It's what Sam just told me." He shifted in the seat so that he was facing her. His left arm was draped across the steering wheel. "Jana, Sam told me there are rumors starting to go around that there's going to be a takeover of my company."

"Takeover?" She gazed at him without comprehension.

Miles nodded and inhaled deeply on his cigarette. "He says they only surfaced a few days ago."

Jana shook her head, trying to understand. "You mean takeover as in *takeover?* Like another company buying up all the stock on the market until they finally gain control?"

"Exactly."

"But . . ." Jana peered intently at him, though in the early-evening darkness she could scarcely see his features. "It isn't true, is it?"

"Certainly not!" Miles exclaimed. "I still personally hold the majority of stock, though we are on the exchange now since I bought that other factory, and we've been negotiating for another one still. But there have been no reports of any other company attempting to buy up large blocks of our stock."

"Then how could such a story get started?" Jana asked in bewilderment. "And why?"

Miles shook his head, flung his half-smoked cigarette out the window, and started the car. "Beats me," he told her. "Unless someone is doing it for political purposes."

"But that's ridiculous," Jana sputtered. "Why, it's way too early yet to even declare yourself formally in the race. Why would someone try to harm you?"

Miles's voice was grim. "Some people will pull any sort of dirty, underhanded scheme to do in the competition. But I agree it seems like extremely early days for such a move by anyone. However, this sort of rumor certainly won't be good for me . . . or for the company. It'll make the employees restless and uneasy, worrying about whether or not their jobs are safe if another outfit suddenly takes control."

Jana suddenly found that she was trembling with anger at the unknown rumormonger. "What can you do to stop it?" she asked as they drove toward home.

Shrugging his shoulders, Miles turned a corner. "For the moment, all I intend to do is ignore it. It might do more harm than good for me to make a public denial . . . adding fuel to the fire, so to speak. Maybe it'll just die a natural death."

"Let's hope so," Jana said fervently.

Miles threw her a quick glance, and there was an odd expression on his face. "If I didn't know better, Mrs. Parrish, I'd almost believe you still cared."

The tone of his voice had been light, and Jana answered him in the same vein, giving him a teasing grin. "Oh, I do, Mr. Parrish, I do. I care about Parrish Manufacturing."

Miles grinned, too, and shook his head. "I knew there had to be a catch."

A week later Jana and Caroline spent the day together shopping for items for Caroline's trousseau. The wedding was only two weeks away. They stopped by the dressmaker's for a fitting of Caroline's going-away suit. Then they visited department stores and boutiques and had a lovely time choosing lacy underwear and nightgowns. Jana insisted upon purchasing for her friend a beautiful amber gown and negligee set trimmed in fine deep brown lace.

"It's gorgeous!" Caroline said enthusiastically, lightly fingering the silky fabric. "I hope Bill will like me in it."

"I imagine," Jana said dryly, "he'll hardly even notice the clothes you wear."

To her amazement, Caroline actually blushed, and then they both laughed. "I suppose," Caroline said, "a married woman ought to know."

Now, to her acute embarrassment, Jana's own face reddened, and her shrewd friend was quick to notice. "How *are* things between you and Miles, anyway, now that you're back?" she asked bluntly.

Jana pretended a suddenly compelling interest in her handbag, which she had opened in order to pull out her checkbook. "Could be better," she answered enigmatically. "Could be worse."

"Which tells me precisely nothing," Caroline said with an edge of exasperation in her voice.

All at once, Jana was angry. "What do you expect me to say?" she demanded. "That everything is marvelous . . . a second honeymoon, complete with

moonlight and roses?" She shook her head. "You
wouldn't believe me, anyway, knowing the real
circumstances of my return."

The salesclerk joined them at the counter then,
and Jana plastered what she hoped was a believably
pleasant smile on her face as she paid the bill. But
her thoughts were on three nights ago when Miles
had glimpsed her in only her half-slip and bra when
she had darted across the hall from her bedroom to
the bathroom. He had been coming down the hall
and had given her a long, measured look, and then
his jaw had clamped together into an angry line.
"Don't ever run around here half naked like that
again!" he had ordered in a clipped voice. "Unless
you're ready to pay the consequences! If we're to
live like brother and sister, then you'd better cover
yourself up decently at all times!"

Since then, the cold aloofness between them had
resumed.

As soon as they were out of the shop and in
Caroline's car, Caroline resumed their discussion.
"Things are pretty bad between you, then?"

Jana pressed her lips tightly together, then nodded
curtly. "Horrible, if you must know. For a little
while I thought . . . well, never mind. Miles loves
Edie, and the sooner we all face that fact, the
happier everyone will be."

"Including you and Guy?"

Jana shrugged. "Well, somebody has to be ex-
pendable in a triangle . . . or should I say quadran-
gle? I'm certain Miles wishes I were at the bottom of
the harbor or something so he'd be free to marry
her." Her eyes suddenly smarted, and she glanced
out the window at the Dock Street Theatre. Her
blurred vision scarcely perceived it, and her mind
was not on the scenery.

"Try not to sound like a complete idiot!" Caroline

chided. "Miles never did love Edie, Jana, and she never loved him, either."

Jana's laugh was ragged and frankly skeptical. "Tell me another fairy tale, friend. If they were never in love, why did they get engaged in the first place?"

"Because," Caroline said patiently as she turned onto the residential street that led to Jana's house, "Edie's dad and ours were good friends, and when her father died he left their finances in dreadful shape. Everybody had always assumed they were wealthy, but in fact they were head over heels in debt. Edie wasn't equipped to deal with such a calamity, and I think Miles felt sorry for her. So . . . they got engaged. But it only lasted a few months, you know, and then they broke it off and she married Guy."

"Apparently there's more between them than pity," Jana reminded as Caroline swept the car into the driveway behind the house. "Have you forgotten that Edie started this whole mess by telling Guy she and Miles *are* having an affair?"

"Hogwash!" Caroline said crudely. "Edie never did tell the truth when a lie would serve her better!"

"But where would be the advantage? So far, all it's done is cause trouble for everybody."

Caroline sighed as they got out of the car, gathered up Jana's packages, and headed for the house. "I don't know what her little game is," she admitted, "but whatever it is, it must have backfired. She called Mom's house yesterday in tears because Guy hasn't sent her support check and she can't pay her bills. Doesn't it just make your heart *bleed?*" she said gleefully. "Apparently Guy won't even talk to her when she calls his office, and he won't answer his phone at his apartment. I say it just serves her

right!" The grin left her face and she sobered.
"However, it's all worrying Mom, of course. She
talked to Guy's secretary a few days ago, and it
sounds as if he's practically never there anymore.
And we can't reach him at his apartment any more
than Edie can."

"You don't think something's happened to him,
do you?" Jana asked anxiously. No matter what the
differences between the two brothers, she had always been fond of her brother-in-law.

Caroline shrugged and made an expressive face.
"If you ask me, he's just going off and brooding
about everything, which is no good, of course, but
who can tell him what to do? He's a grown man. I
just hope he'll show up at my wedding and not pick a
scene with Miles."

Jana hoped so, too. It would be dreadful if Caroline's wedding were ruined because of Miles's and
Guy's hostility toward each other. And it would be
equally hurtful to Caroline if one or the other of
them were absent on her big day.

Not that Miles would actually skip it, though, she
told herself later that afternoon after Caroline had
gone and she had undressed to take a bath before
dinner. Miles, as her older brother, had the honor of
walking Caroline down the aisle that day, while Guy
was supposed to be one of the ushers. Jana smiled as
she stepped into the warm, perfumed bathwater.
Caroline was upset that Jana could not be her
matron of honor. But when she had first made her
wedding plans, Jana had still been in Atlanta and
Caroline had not believed she would come back and
face Miles at the wedding. So Caroline had asked
other girlfriends to be her attendants. At this late
date, the best Jana could do was preside over the
guest book, a job Caroline scorned as being unwor-

thy of her best friend, but which Jana honestly did not mind at all. The thing that really bothered her was the knowledge that Edie was to be one of the bridesmaids. She had been asked long before the split with Guy, and her gown was already made. It was too late for her to bow out now.

Impatient with herself, Jana thrust aside all thoughts of Edie. There was no point in dwelling on unpleasantness and only making herself miserable.

After her bath, she dressed in a long floral-print dress that was as comfortable as it was pretty. It was exactly the thing for an evening at home, she decided as she stood before the mirror and brushed mascara onto her eyelashes.

A few minutes later she went into the kitchen, from which came delicious smells that teased at her stomach. Daisy was there, just shrugging her ample bulk into her coat. When she saw Jana, she said, "There's a chicken-and-rice casserole in the oven, Mrs. Parrish, broccoli in that pan on top of the stove, and there's a fruit salad in the refrigerator."

"It sounds wonderful, Daisy." Jana smiled. "Thank you. Have a nice evening."

After the woman left, Jana went into the living room and, glancing at the clock on the mantel, decided it was not too early to mix the drinks. Miles should be coming home soon.

She had just finished and picked up her own and was about to sit down when the front door opened and Miles came in.

"Hi," she said, keeping her voice light and casual as he shed his jacket. "I've got your drink made. How was your day?"

"Horrible," Miles replied as he sank wearily into a chair.

Jana carried his drink to him and, for the first

time, really looked at him. Lines of tension and fatigue were etched around his eyes and mouth and across his forehead. His eyes were dark and dull, as though perhaps he had a headache.

"What's wrong?" she asked quietly as she sat down on the end of the sofa nearest him.

Miles sipped at his drink, then took a deep breath. "First, a lot of the employees were out sick today. The flu or something seems to be raging through town like a fire. Then, one of the machines broke down, and it can't be fixed until we get some new parts for it. And on top of all that, Sam wasn't kidding about that rumor. It's all over the factory, and I can sense the disquiet in the air. There seems to be an addition to the rumor as well. I pumped Kathleen, and she told me she's heard I'm in financial difficulties and may even have to lay off workers."

"If it's that bad, you're going to have to put a stop to it, Miles. And fast!" Jana said decisively.

"Got any ideas?" he asked in a tired voice. Absently, he rubbed his neck, as though it were stiff.

Without even thinking, Jana set her glass on the coffee table, got up and went around behind him, and began massaging his neck and shoulders. It was something she had often done in the past.

"I think it's best," she said thoughtfully as her fingers pressed gently against his tightly corded muscles, "that you face this thing head on."

"Umm, that's good. Yes, there," Miles said with satisfaction. He bent his head forward so that her fingers might have better access to his neck. Then he added, "You always did like total directness."

Jana smiled. "Dorothy said something like that the day I came back, something about my liking all the cards on the table, face up. It's true, I do; and in this case I think it's the only way you're going to ease the situation. Either write a letter to be given to each employee or call a general meeting, but tell them, Miles, so they'll stop worrying." Her hands, working across his shoulders, felt the gradual relaxation of taut muscles, as though a stretched rubber band were slowly being released to return to its natural state.

"You're right," he said after a moment. "You're absolutely right. I'll do it."

Suddenly, one of her hands was captured by a large, browned one. Jana went still, and then, slowly, still retaining his grip on her hand, Miles pulled her around the chair and down onto his lap.

Jana's heart lurched. Her silvery gray eyes met the warm, brown abyss of his, and as the gaze between them lengthened she had the oddest sensation of floating on the liquid current of his vision. She felt as though his gaze were a dark sea that, while holding her captive by its bottomless depths, would always keep her safe and secure.

Shaken and mesmerized, Jana could not move. Miles's face was very close to hers. He continued to look at her, almost as though he were trying to memorize her features. At last he ended the paralyzing stillness when he bent his head and his lips took possession of hers.

Miles pulled her back until she lay against his chest. Without any realization of doing so, Jana's hand crept to his shoulder and clung there as their lips parted and moved to accept each other. An old, familiar passion flared between them.

A need, a desperate yearning that had been submerged for so many months, now came raging through Jana like a dangerous fever. Her entire body quivered with aching longing. Miles's hand slid up from her waist to caress her breast through the silky fabric of her dress. She was unaware of a tiny, betraying moan of desire that escaped from her throat. Her own hand had gradually lowered from his shoulder to his firm chest and by touch alone had worked open one of the buttonholes on his shirt. Her fingers slid inside to thrill to the warmth of his skin and to delight in the crisp roughness of the hair centered below his breastbone.

Slowly, Miles's mouth released hers. The burning heat that flamed in his eyes could only be a reflection of what must be in her own. His hard, chiseled lips had softened incredibly. "We always could ignite an inferno in each other, precious heart," he said in a husky, sensuous voice. "This game we've been playing of staying apart in the same house simply can't continue, you know."

"I know," Jana whispered, unable to be anything less than totally honest.

"I want you, Jana," Miles said softly. One of his fingers was brushing back and forth across her cheek, sending tantalizing little thrills through her. "I want to make love to you right now. Let's bury the past and start over from tonight."

Jana nodded. "Yes," she replied. Emotion made her voice unsteady. "It . . . it's what I want, too."

Now Miles laughed, exuberant and eager. "Then what are we waiting for, Mrs. Parrish?"

"Well, it's early yet," she teased, "and Daisy's dinner will be spoiled if we don't—"

"To hell with dinner!" Miles growled, pretending anger as his arms tightened around her. "The only appetite I've got right now is for you. And after all these months without you, I don't intend to wait a minute longer. Not now, when I've got you back in my arms at last!"

Jana laughed and slid off his lap, dashing for the

stairs. "What are *you* waiting for, slowpoke?" she jeered.

She only made it to the second stair before Miles reached her, caught her roughly against his chest, and gave her another long kiss.

When they entered the bedroom, Jana paused. Since her return she had very carefully avoided the room they had previously shared, because she had known the memories would be too painful; but now she gazed around it fondly, forgetting old hurts as Miles's strong arm remained firmly around her waist. The room was exactly as she remembered it, with the large bed against the center of one wall. Opposite it were the massive dresser and bureau. Another wall had an opened doorway that led to the bathroom and small dressing room and walk-in closets. Though it was an old house, the previous owners had renovated it so that it was thoroughly comfortable for modern-day living. This room, with its peach-colored walls and white woodwork, had always been Jana's favorite.

She was not allowed to admire the room for long. Forcefully reminding her of his presence, Miles pulled her into his arms again. As he reached behind her, unzipping her dress, his lips were planting tiny kisses on her eyelids, her cheeks, her earlobes, her chin, her pulsating throat. It was as though he were dropping minuscule seeds into the soil to grow to fruition in a warm spring sun.

Jana had no false modesty about appearing naked before him after Miles had undressed her. She reveled in the glowing admiration in his eyes, and his gaze stirred her own desires for him. How many lonely nights she had remembered that expression in his eyes and ached to see it again, believing she never would.

Their coming together was a frenzied, wild, total

abandonment to the cravings of their bodies. Miles stroked her smooth, pale skin, knowing exactly where and when to touch her to arouse her to a delirious pitch. As his fingers roamed from her breasts down to her hips Jana's fingernails dug into his shoulders and she quivered with glorious expectancy.

At last their desperate needs were appeased and they lay, limp and silent, with arms across each other's middles, in contented fatigue.

"Jana?" Miles finally broke the stillness.

"Mmmm?"

"It can work for us again, you know. Our marriage. If we try . . . and have trust in each other."

"Trust?" She repeated the word in a curious voice, as though she were unsure of its meaning. Now reality was returning, intruding, and with it sharp, clear memory.

Miles's arm tightened around her and his voice was low. "I'm asking you to trust me in the future . . . for both our sakes. Two people simply can't reach such heights together as we just did and *not* be able to make a success of their marriage . . . if they want it badly enough."

"And you do?" The words trembled on Jana's lips, and she was furious with herself.

Miles surprised her by laughing, dispelling the seriousness of a moment ago. "Want me to prove all over again just how badly I do?" He nibbled at her earlobe, and his hand slid upward from her flat stomach to cover one soft breast again.

"No, you don't!" Jana shoved him away and rolled swiftly to the edge of the bed. "Maybe you *still* don't want any dinner, but I'm starved!" She got to her feet and fled toward the bathroom.

Behind her, Miles chuckled. The timbre of his

voice was deep and rich and infinitely pleasant to the ears. "Now," he said with an air of great puzzlement, "I wonder what could have possibly given you such a ravenous appetite?"

On Caroline's wedding day, Jana realized that ever since that night Miles had come home tired and disturbed and they had ended by making love, she had been living in a fool's paradise. Miles was wonderfully attentive to her. They had picked up the old habits and routines of their marriage just as though there had never been an interruption. But on the beautiful Saturday afternoon when, in the same famous and lovely old church where they had been married themselves, Caroline walked down the aisle beside Miles, Jana admitted to herself the one thing she had been avoiding. Though they were living together again intimately as man and wife, and though deep within her own heart she had faced the truth that she had never stopped loving Miles for so much as a single instant, he had not said he still loved her.

And the reason, she thought unhappily, was now standing at the altar along with the other bridesmaids. It was the first time Jana had seen Edie since her return to Charleston, and she could not dislodge the bitter lump of pain that choked her throat. Edie's blond beauty was glowing today, enhanced by the pale sea-green chiffon gown she wore. Her dazzling looks made the other bridesmaids seem to pale into insignificance beside her. How *could* she stand there and smile so charmingly, so innocently, Jana wondered, when she had wreaked havoc in so many lives?

Now she glanced to the right of the altar, where Bill Kirby stood awaiting his bride. But Jana was not looking at the groom. Instead, she watched Guy and noted the grim line to his jaw as he, in turn, gazed at his estranged wife.

Jana sighed. At least Guy had shown up, which had been a matter of speculation right up until an hour ago. Miles had said that Guy had not attended the rehearsal the previous evening. Jana hoped that they would all be able to get through this day somehow without any outward unpleasantness.

As Miles and Caroline reached the altar Dorothy groped for Jana's hand. Jana knew instinctively that the older woman was just as worried as she was.

However, Guy and Miles carefully kept a wide distance between each other at the reception. At least, Jana thought gratefully as she observed them from her vantage point behind the guest-book table, they're determined to keep peace for Caroline's and Dorothy's sakes.

She had not expected Edie to seek her out, and she tensed with distaste when the other girl approached her.

"Hello, Jana," Edie said sweetly, with the brightest of smiles. "I heard you had come back to Miles."

"That's right." Jana clenched her teeth and pressed her lips against them in what she hoped would pass as a smile. "How are you, Edie?"

Edie shrugged her shoulders in a so-so gesture, picked up the pen from the table, and signed the guest book with a flourish. "I suppose," she went on, "when you heard Miles might run for Congress, you couldn't wait to get back so that you'll be able to bask in all the glamour and glory of it yourself."

Before Jana could even begin to frame a reply to such an unexpected and ridiculous charge, Edie nodded pleasantly and walked away.

Jana thrust the nasty little comment from her mind as guests came and placed their names in the book. She smiled and chatted and actually even managed to completely forget about Edie as the celebration progressed through the afternoon.

But later she was jolted into unwelcome awareness again. She had just gotten herself a cup of punch and was walking across the room to speak to an old school friend of hers and Caroline's when she saw Guy standing near an opened doorway. There was a distinct scowl on his face, and as she passed close behind him Jana glanced curiously through the doorway herself. All at once her blood froze in her veins.

In the other room Miles and Edie were standing close together, intent in an earnest conversation, totally oblivious of their surroundings or of the possibility that they might be observed. It was as though an invisible magic circle held them together, separating them from the rest of the world.

Sickening nausea assailed Jana's stomach. She turned abruptly and walked away, head held high, shoulders straight, a carefully arranged bland expression on her face. No one, she told herself fiercely, would ever know how much she was hurting inside or how hopeless her future appeared.

Chapter Four

The chandelier glittered above the elegantly appointed table in the formal dining room of the house on East Battery. Fine Irish lace covered the oval table and set off to perfection the Wedgwood china, the crystal goblets, and the highly polished silver. Candles in their silver holders flickered from the center of the table on either side of a floral arrangement.

"She was a beautiful bride."

"She shouldn't have been there."

"She did look gorgeous. I hope she'll be happy."

"Why shouldn't she have been there? Because *you* say so?"

"I wonder where she is now," Dorothy mused.

"I hope I never see her again," Guy said fervently.

Dorothy's blue eyes darkened with disbelief as she stared across the table at her son. "You *what?*" she exclaimed. "Why, Guy, I thought you loved your sister!"

Guy stared back, and there was equal disbelief on his face. "My sister? Who's talking about her? I'm talking about my ex-wife!" He scowled as his brooding eyes surveyed his brother. "I'm sure the only reason she stayed in the wedding party was so she'd have a good excuse to see Miles again . . . as though they needed to find excuses to see each other!"

"She's not your ex-wife yet," Miles said in a grim voice, "and I never find excuses to see her! She's all yours, Guy! I don't want her!"

"Oh, you don't?" Guy's voice was bitter. "All you wanted was to take her away from me and now you're through with her, is that it?"

A hissing sound of exasperation whistled between Miles's clenched teeth, and his hands on the table doubled into fists. "How many times do I have to tell you, Guy . . . I've never touched your wife! And I'm getting extremely tired of the accusations!"

Jana placed her own hand over one of Miles's. "Stop it!" she ordered in a low voice. "Both of you! Look at the way you're upsetting your mother!"

They all looked toward Dorothy, and indeed her turmoil was obvious. She still wore the elegant blue gown she had worn at her daughter's wedding earlier in the day. Though her bearing was almost regal as she presided at the head of her dining table, her face had paled to the color of rice parchment and tears were swimming in her eyes.

"I'm sorry, Mother," Miles said contritely. "I was hoping this could be a pleasant day for you and that Guy and I could bury our differences for your sake."

Guy said nothing as he gazed intently at his plate, but there was a flushed, shamed expression staining his cheeks and brow.

Jana, who had unconsciously been holding her
breath, slowly expelled it and reached for her wine.
She knew her own color was heightened from reaction to the turbulent scene, from her own private
torments, and now she prayed no one would notice.

She wished that Dorothy had not insisted on this
little family dinner after the wedding. She understood the reasons very well. It would give them a
chance to relax after all the excitement, and opportunity to rehash the event. For Dorothy, it would fill
an otherwise very empty and lonely evening. She
must be feeling a bit sad and despondent now that
Caroline was married and would be living away from
her in another city. She needed the rest of her family
to fill the void.

But Jana had known instinctively that it was a
mistake. How could it be otherwise, she asked
herself, with the brothers at each other's throats like
this? Miles had told his mother he had hoped he and
Guy could get through the day without airing their
hostilities. But then, Miles did not know that Guy
had witnessed him alone in that anteroom with Edie.
Miles had no idea what either of them had seen.

From beneath her thick fringe of lashes, Jana
glanced across at Guy and felt a stir of kinship with
him that went far beyond any family ties. Guy was
deeply hurt, and so was she. She could perfectly
understand the rage and resentment that were gnaw-
ing away at him like a hideous disease. He loved
Edie very much. It was as simple as that. Otherwise,
he would not be so angry. He was suffering in exactly
the same manner Jana had suffered when she had
first discovered Miles and Edie together . . . and
was still suffering, in fact.

Even now she ached inside with a pain that was as
unrelenting as it was severe. Why must she still love
Miles? she wondered despondently as she toyed with

her dinner. It was all so unfair, so very unfair. She gazed without appetite at the baked quail and *petits pois* on her plate.

Since that night they had made love, Jana had been absurdly hopeful that they could indeed salvage their marriage. She had hoped that eventually Miles would be as much in love with her as he had seemed to be when they had first married. But today, seeing him with Edie, the hope had crumbled like ashes from a burning log. No matter what Miles said to the contrary, he *did* still want his brother's wife.

The thought sickened Jana, and she placed her fork on her plate and gave up all pretense of eating. She wanted nothing so much as for this dinner to end, for this day to end, so that she could lick her wounds in private. Unlike Guy, she was carefully concealing her own emotions beneath a placid demeanor. But she did not think she could keep on doing so much longer.

"Jana?"

She was jolted back to an awareness of her surroundings by Miles's sharp voice. When she lifted her head, she found his dark gaze penetrating as he studied her. Embarrassed, she realized that Dorothy's maid stood at her elbow, waiting to learn if she was finished with her plate.

Summoning a smile, she nodded her assent, and the maid removed the unwanted plate.

"Are you all right?" Dorothy asked with concern.

"I'm fine," Jana said. "I was just lost in thought, I suppose."

"About what?" Miles inquired.

She shrugged her shoulders and refused to meet his eyes. "Nothing much," she lied.

"Mom," Guy said abruptly, "if you'll excuse me, I think I'll skip dessert. I'm tired and I'd like to go home early." He pushed back his chair and went around the table, where he bent down to kiss Dorothy's cheek.

Dorothy grabbed his hand. "Call me sometime this week," she insisted. "It's been very difficult to reach you lately."

Dull color suffused Guy's face again. "I've had a lot on my mind, as you well know." He straightened, patted his mother's hand, and added, "But I'll call you soon, I promise. Good night, Mom. Good night, Jana." Without a glance toward Miles, he quickly left the room.

"Go after him, Miles," Dorothy pleaded. "Make peace with your brother."

Miles's face became stony. "There's nothing I'd like better, Mother, believe me. But he won't listen. You heard him tonight. He's determined to believe Edie's story."

"But if it isn't true, why would she even say such a dreadful thing?" Dorothy asked in sad confusion.

"Heaven only knows," Miles snapped impatiently, "because I certainly don't! Let's change the subject, Mom. I don't want to talk about it anymore, and until Guy calms down there's just no use in trying to reason with him."

It was another hour before Miles and Jana could leave. The three of them dawdled over coffee and small talk until Jana's nerves jangled like a rattling chain. She nursed her throbbing temples and tried not to squirm in her chair as Dorothy seemed to go on endlessly about the wedding and every guest present. Miles, with uncharacteristic patience, listened, and nodded at all the right places.

But at last they took their leave, drove the short distance to their own house, and went inside. Miles flipped on the hall light so that they could see their way as they mounted the stairs. Jana lifted the hem of her fawn-colored dress and preceded him.

Miles yawned as they entered the bedroom and began tugging at the bow tie at his throat. "It's been a long day," he said sleepily. "I'm glad the festivities are finally over, aren't you?"

"Yes." Jana did not look at him as she went over to the bed, sat down on the edge, and began unbuckling the heeled sandals she wore. As soon as she had them off, she scooped both shoes up by the back straps and dangled them from two fingers, then headed toward the dressing room, where she dropped the shoes carelessly into a corner instead of wrapping them in tissue paper and restoring them to their original box as she normally did. Tonight she was past caring about anything, much less a pair of shoes.

In robot fashion, she moved over to stand in front of the dressing-table mirror and began removing the diamond earrings and necklace she wore . . . the same earrings and necklace Miles had presented to her on their wedding day. She had worn them today as a sort of talisman—as though if worn to Caroline's wedding they would somehow bring about the total commitment she yearned to renew in her own marriage.

What a joke! she thought bitterly as she dropped one earring into the opened jewelry box on the table. The marriage vows Caroline and Bill had exchanged today had been beautiful and sincere, while the vows between herself and Miles had long ago lost their sparkling purity. They were tarnished vows now, ugly and rusted like the metal hulk of a ship long sunk in the Atlantic.

The second earring joined its mate in the jewelry box, and Jana raised her hands behind her neck to unhook the latch on the necklace. Her eyes lifted once more to her own reflection in the mirror, and it gave her Miles's image as well. Silently, he had come to stand just behind her.

He had shed both the tie and the black tuxedo jacket. Now the formal ruffled shirtfront hung open, exposing the hard breadth of his chest and the furry hair that curled there.

Their eyes met, and little flames danced in his. *Why does he have to be so good-looking?* The question flitted across Jana's mind. *And why does his nearness make me feel so weak, so giddy?*

Miles's hands went up to cover hers at her shoulders. Slowly, he bent his head, and his lips traced a delicate pattern across the back of her neck, sending tingling little sensations rippling through her. Jana squeezed her eyes shut, as though if she blocked out the sight of him she would also be able to block out the desire that his nearness always elicited from her.

A zipping sound and his warm breath against her bare shoulder told her he was starting to undress her. Jana clutched at the front of the dress in defense. Then Miles's lips were moving lightly across her back.

She quivered. "No." Her voice was thin and, to her dismay, lacked firm conviction.

"Don't be silly, precious heart," Miles murmured. His hands went up to remove the hairpins that bound her hair in a mass of curls at the crown of her head. The silky brown locks came crashing down to swirl and eddy around her shoulders like dark, billowing waves. Miles entangled his fingers through the finely textured mass and then gently turned her around to face him. His hands pried hers from their grip on the bodice of her dress, and an instant later it slithered to her feet.

He took possession of her vulnerable lips, his kiss teasing and light as his hands now went to her back again to unhook her bra. As though in slow motion, Miles slid the straps down her shoulders and arms, and in a moment more it, too, fell unheeded to the floor.

Protestingly, Jana's hands strained against his warm chest. But the heat that penetrated her touch sent a furor of longing through every nerve in her body. Her senses became a whirlpool of dizzying, aching need, and she was drowning as her body, of its own accord, responded to his caressing hands as they stroked her breasts.

With passionate force Miles parted her lips with his and his tongue sought the warm, moist interior of hers, sending new sensations of liquid desire burning through her veins.

"Let's go to bed," he whispered at last as he lifted his head to gaze down at her. A gleam of smoldering ardor flared in his dark eyes. The tender expression there and the softening of his lips were almost Jana's undoing . . . that and the exciting things his hands were doing to her body, which was responding to him with treacherous longing.

With an effort that took all the willpower she possessed, Jana once again pushed against his chest, separating them by scant inches. "No." Her voice was thick and husky, but at least this time it contained the firmness it needed.

Miles still held her in a loose embrace, his arms around her waist, his hands touching the bare skin of her back. She felt him stiffen in surprise even before the tender light was extinguished in his eyes.

"Why?" The one word was hoarse and filled with disbelief.

His arms dropped away from her, leaving her skin suddenly chilled. Jana trembled as she stepped back to put more space between their aroused bodies.

Her arms came up to cross in front of her, shielding her breasts from him.

Her head gave a short, negative shake, and she had to fight against the compulsion to gaze at the floor instead of at him. She chewed at her lower lip in agitation, and then she looked straight at him and lifted her chin in unconscious pride.

"I'm not going to sleep with you again, Miles," she stated flatly.

Bewilderment clouded his eyes as he stared at her. "But why?" he asked again. "These last couple of weeks we—"

"It's over," Jana interrupted. Her voice hardened. "I saw you today at the wedding . . . off in that other room alone with Edie. So did Guy. So do you wonder that he doesn't believe you when you say there's nothing between you? I don't believe you, either. Besides, I had proof with my own eyes months ago."

"If you don't believe me"—now Miles's voice, too, was hard and unyielding—"then why have you let me make love to you since you came back? Why, Jana, if you hate me so much?"

She half turned from him, unable to go on looking at him, knowing that if she did the tears would come. Above all, she must not let him know how deeply she was hurt, must not let him see the love in her eyes.

"I was a *fool!*" Her voice vibrated with intense emotion. "I was weak! But let me make this plain, Miles. I have no intention of behaving so weakly or foolishly again. Not ever!"

"Would you . . ." Miles seemed to be struggling to calm his own turbulent anger. "Would you be interested in hearing an explanation? Of why I was talking with Edie today . . . of what really happened that day you walked out on me?"

Jana's laugh was bitter and scornful. "No, thank you. What is already clear requires no explanations."

Taking her by complete surprise, Miles jerked her around to face him. Black anger narrowed his eyes, tightened his jaw, and his chest heaved as he breathed heavily. For one brief instant, Jana physically feared him, for the glint in his eyes spoke of dangerous depths that were rising swiftly to the surface.

"All right," he grated in a low, deep voice. "Have it your way! No explanations wanted, none given! Pack your bags again and go, *wife!*" The word fell from his sneering lips, sounding ugly and vulgar. "I have no desire for a marriage that isn't a marriage, for a wife who has no trust, for a woman who plays hot and cold games according to a moment's whim! Leave me, Jana! Tonight!"

Now she was furious again and forgot her fear of him. "Your constant references to trust are laughable, Miles. They really are, considering you're the one who killed the trust I once had in you!" She gave a sharp shake to her head, and her hair swished violently against her shoulders. "All the same, I'm staying until next year after the election. I promised Dorothy," she reminded him pointedly.

"Then I just won't even get into the race!" Miles snapped. "That way you won't have that excuse anymore."

"Fine!" Jana almost shouted. "You tell Dorothy that, and I'll be happy to pack my bags and go. But tonight I'm tired and sleepy and I'm going to bed . . . in the spare room. So will you *please* get out of here and let me get ready?"

Miles gave her a mocking half salute. "Be happy to," he said in a taunting voice, "because, as it happens, I've completely lost all interest in your alluring body." Contemptuously, his gaze swept down her still partially nude body. "I have no more desire than the next man to cuddle up with a block of ice."

Jana winced when she happened to catch a glimpse of herself in the bathroom mirror the next morning. Her hair was tangled, attesting to the hours spent tossing in bed all night, and there were dark smudges circling her eyes. Even her skin appeared sallow, as though she had been through a long illness instead of only a sleepless night.

She showered and carefully applied makeup to hide the ravages of unhappiness. Then, wrapping herself in a towel, she walked down the hall into Miles's room, the one she no longer shared with him. Her clothes were still in the dressing-room closet there. But she did not worry that he would suddenly appear and see her in her scanty attire, because it was already well past ten and he never slept that late.

She was right. The bedroom was empty, and she was able to dress in complete privacy and without any need for haste. She pulled on a pair of beige pants and a lighter-hued beige long-sleeved top. Then she tackled her hair, brushing it ruthlessly until at last it hung freely against her shoulders, silky and smooth.

It was as quiet downstairs as it had been upstairs, and as Jana went toward the kitchen she realized that Miles must have gone out. Which was fine with her, she thought with relief. After the stormy scene between them the night before, she felt ill equipped to face him as tired as she was this morning.

There was coffee already made, and a used coffee cup on the counter told its silent story. Though he had made coffee, Miles must have gone off without any breakfast, because there were no other signs that the kitchen had been occupied before her.

Jana had no appetite, either. She settled instead for two cups of coffee to awaken and fortify her for the day ahead. But as she sipped at the second cup she felt a sudden and compelling urge to get out of the house herself. Why, she asked herself, should she stay here and wait for Miles to return? After all, they would probably only quarrel again. Moreover, she was in no mood to talk to Dorothy today either, and her mother-in-law would probably telephone after she returned home from church services.

Jana drained her cup and set it down on the counter beside its twin. She ran from the room and upstairs, where she snatched her purse and then raced down again.

Miles's car was missing from the garage, as she had expected, and she walked purposefully toward her own. But with a lightning change of decision, she turned and left the garage. Today she wanted to be cooped up in a car no more than she wanted to be imprisoned by the silent walls of the house.

Her footsteps took her briskly down the street. It was a gloriously clear day, and sunlight sparkled on the windowpanes of the houses she passed. The morning air was cool. Fleetingly, Jana wished she had thought to wear a sweater, but before long the effort of walking warmed her.

When she reached Atlantic Street she turned, and in only a few more minutes she arrived at the seawall along East Battery. A number of tourists were already strolling along the seawall, and she mingled with them, feeling a sudden freedom in being among strangers, even though she was only a short walk away from Dorothy Parrish's home. But just now she gave no thought to the nearby house where she had first met Miles. She was intent only on this moment, realizing it was the first time she had truly relaxed in weeks.

She now stood near the point of the peninsula on which the city was built, where the Ashley and Cooper rivers flowed together to form the harbor. A gusty breeze whipped at her hair, blowing it away from her face. The combination of stiff breeze and warm sun felt invigorating, and Jana lifted her face in silent appreciation.

In the distance Fort Sumter was clearly visible. Entering the harbor from its dock on the Ashley River was a tour boat, teeming with sightseers who would soon be walking around on the island fort. In addition, the harbor today was speckled with the bright colors of sailboats as residents took advantage of such a beautiful weekend day.

For a long while Jana stayed on the waterfront, enjoying the tangy air and watching the boaters. She allowed her mind to rest, but finally her thoughts began to intrude once more, clamoring insistently for attention. Still resistant, she turned and headed toward the old downtown section of the graceful city.

She walked for hours, heedless of the miles as she tramped past historic buildings like the Heyward-Washington House, where George Washington had once been a guest, and the Four Corners of Law. She finally wound up on Market Street, which was strewn with shops and restaurants and even an outdoor flea market. But though she strolled and meandered up one street and down another, Jana paid scant attention to her surroundings. Her thoughts refused to be banished any longer, no matter how far she went or how fast she walked to escape them.

Miles had told her to leave and that, in order to force her to do so, he would give up his aspirations for the Senate. He detested her that much, wanted her out of his life that badly! The pain of it was excruciating. He loved Edie so passionately that he did not care what it cost his brother, his mother, his own political future, much less what it did to her!

And yet he had become angry with her because she had refused to allow him to make love to her. Jana's mouth pressed into a line of bitterness. As long as she had been foisted back on him, Miles had decided to take advantage of the situation. Though he no longer loved her, she still obviously held a certain physical appeal. For him, that must be enough, while for her their lovemaking had been an expression of her love for him.

How she hated herself for being so weak as to still love him! Where was her pride, her self-respect? Scornfully, she jeered at herself. If she were any kind of real woman, she would have stopped loving Miles Parrish the very instant she had discovered him in the arms of someone else. If she really had respect for herself, she would have put him firmly out of her heart forever. She would never have allowed him to touch her again.

Dusk was descending over the majestic old houses when Jana finally retraced her steps along the street where Miles's house stood. *And it is his house,* she thought as she paused before it in the waning afternoon light. *I left it once, and I'll have to leave it again.* True, legally it belonged to them both, but she knew that, without Miles, for her the house would only be an empty shell. As her heart was now.

Fatigue from the long hours of walking began to catch up with her as she climbed the steps. Her stomach also felt slightly queasy, and for the first time it dawned on her that she had forgotten to eat all day.

She opened the door and walked inside. Miles stood beside the Queen Anne desk, the white telephone receiver in his hand. The instant he saw her, he violently slammed it down. In one fluid movement he was in front of her, his hands clamping her arms like a vise.

"*Where* in the devil have you been?" he growled from deep in his throat. He gave her a rough shake, so that her head vibrated. "I've been worried to death! I was just calling the police to see if they had any reports about an injured or sick woman being found!"

Jana's eyes widened in amazement at the intensity of his anxiety, at the livid anger that darkened his features and blazed from his eyes. "You're hurting me!" she gasped, struggling to free herself from his punishing grip.

Miles released her immediately and glared at her. "Answer me!" he commanded arrogantly. "Where have you been all this time?"

Resentfully, Jana glared back at him and rubbed her sore arms. There would probably be ugly bruises by morning.

"I went for a walk!" she snapped, turning from him and going toward the stairs. "And, anyway, I don't see why you're so worked up about it. You were gone this morning without bothering to let me know where you went. Not," she added heatedly, "that I can't make a good guess!"

One of her arms was trapped again by powerful fingers, and the action jerked Jana to a halt. "Meaning what?" Miles seethed as he spun her around to face him.

"Exactly what you think I mean!" Jana snapped. "It was a lovely day today, wasn't it? I imagine the beach on Kiawah Island was especially beautiful."

To her utter astonishment, Miles suddenly threw back his head and roared with laughter. Jana, however, saw nothing amusing and continued to scowl sullenly.

Finally the chuckling subsided. "Sorry to disappoint you, precious heart, but I wasn't with Edie this morning—and, what's more, I've got plenty of witnesses to prove it." He paused dramatically, cocked an amused eyebrow at her, and intoned solemnly, "I was in church."

Jana's mouth fell open and she gaped at him. "Church?" Her voice came out squeaky, like a mouse's.

He nodded, and a tiny grin twitched his lips. "Church. I took Mom. She called this morning and asked me to go with her. I was going to invite you along as well, but when I peeked in at you, you were dead to the world and snoring loud enough to shake the windows."

"You're lying!"

"About going to church?" he asked innocently.

"About my snoring!" she exclaimed. "I don't!"

Miles grinned broadly now, took her by the hand, and led her toward the sofa, where he unceremoniously thrust her down and then sat down beside her. "I *was* lying last night when I told you I wanted you to go, Jana. I said it because I was furious with you. But today, when I found you gone, even though you hadn't taken your clothes or your car, I was worried sick when you didn't come back." The grin had faded, and now he was truly serious. "You made it plain enough last night that you don't want me anymore, that our marriage isn't going to work. I'll accept that. But I would very much appreciate it if you'd stay . . . for Mother's sake. She's been hurt enough lately."

"Then you're going ahead with your plans to run for office?"

Miles's eyes were fathomless as they met hers in steady regard. "It depends on you," he said quietly. "If you'll stay, I will."

Jana saw that he meant it. Miles, like his mother and his father before him, was imbued with Parrish family pride: a Parrish did not air his problems in public. If she left him now, he would not face the close scrutiny of his life that all politicians must endure. It would, in some instances, overshadow his objectives, his beliefs, and cast doubts in voters' minds of his ability to handle their interests capably. And in spite of their serious problems on a personal level, Jana knew with absolute certainty that the state needed such dedicated and responsible representation as a man like Miles could provide. Never had she known him to shirk any duty, however large or burdensome it might be, and that was one of the things about him that she had always most admired. Also, Miles had inherited from his father a strong sense of civic duty. He truly believed that every person owed some form of service to his country in exchange for all the comforts and benefits derived. He felt that, though there were many things wrong in government, there was no excuse to complain if one was not willing to work toward a better solution.

She sighed heavily. "I'll stay."

"Good girl!" Miles flashed her a beaming smile. "In that case," he asked appealingly, "will you attend a civic-club dinner with me tomorrow night? I'm the guest speaker, and it would be nice to have you there for moral support."

"Whoops! Here we go!" Jana laughed. "I forgot to tell you, what with all the wedding excitement, but yesterday morning I got a phone call asking me to address a women's club meeting in a couple of weeks."

"The topic?" Miles inquired with avid curiosity.

She grinned at him. "My husband's position on women's rights issues, of course. What else?" She spread out her hands. "So . . . what *is* your position, Mr. Parrish?"

Miles returned the grin. "Well, speaking as the husband of a *very* liberated lady, I guess I'll have to be for them! By the way, our personnel director is leaving in a couple of months. Do you want your old job back when he goes?"

"Love it," she answered promptly. "It'll give me an excellent excuse not to accept any more women's club speeches. But why is Bob leaving? I thought you said he was doing a super job."

Miles nodded. "He is. That's why I'm sending him to Columbia to take over the same duties at the other plant."

"And the one there?"

He shook his head. "There never was one, formally. The assistant manager handled it, and I just never got around to hiring anyone new to fill the position."

They attended the dinner the following evening. In spite of herself, Jana felt proud of Miles as he took the podium and made his speech. He looked so dignified, strong, and vital in the charcoal gray suit and burgundy tie she had laid out for him earlier in the evening. His resonant voice was pleasant as he spoke, yet punctuated now and then with vigor as he drove home some important point.

Only two evenings later there was yet another dinner and another speech, this one before an environmental group. Earlier in the day Jana had gone out and purchased a new dress with a matching jacket in peach-blossom silk. She had shaken her head regretfully over the outrageous price tag, but at the same time she considered it in the nature of a business expense. Now that Miles was actively engaged in public appearances, as his wife she must look her best.

. Before Miles arrived home from the office, she again laid out his clothes across the bed, this time a dark navy suit with a pale blue tie. She chose a silver tie clasp and cuff links and placed them on the dresser where he could easily find them. Then she went to her own room to dress.

They had called a mute cease-fire to their quarrels ever since the night of Caroline's wedding and had resumed the little married things they had always done for each other—like her laying out his clothes and mixing his evening drink. Miles, in turn, made her a cup of hot tea each evening before bedtime. He had started buying her miniature collector's items again, a habit he had begun shortly after their honeymoon. Jana had always taken pleasure in her small treasures; there was a special display case in their dining room that contained the porcelain thimbles and tiny ceramic and china dishes he had given her. But even though they were both attempting to make their marriage normal in an outward way by a show of thoughtfulness and consideration of each other, since that fateful night Jana had slept alone in the guest room and Miles had not once approached her.

Tonight, in addition to making his prepared speech to the group he had gone to address, Miles also got some attention from the press. Present were both TV and newspaper reporters. After the dinner was over, they approached Miles and Jana.

Completely surprising them, one of the reporters said, "Mr. Parrish, we've heard there's the possibility of a takeover of your company by a larger conglomerate. Is your factory in difficult financial straits, sir?"

Annoyance came and went so fast across Miles's face that only Jana was aware of it as he gave an unruffled negative reply. "Our company is in excellent financial condition, and there's absolutely no truth in that rumor. In fact, we're one of the few smaller companies in the area right now that is hiring new employees and increasing production."

The television reporter turned to Jana. "Mrs. Parrish, how do you feel about the idea of your husband running for Congress?"

Jana smiled. "I'm all for it. I believe my husband can do a lot of good for this state and the nation, just as his father did during his years in the Senate."

"Thank you." The reporter turned back to Miles with another question, and Jana sighed with relief that she had been let off the hook so quickly.

A few minutes later they were able to leave at last, and as they drove homeward Jana voiced her concern. "*Who* can be spreading these rumors, Miles, and how did that reporter get wind of them?"

He shook his head. "I wish to heaven I knew. I thought I'd squashed the matter at the factory after I called the assembly and told them it wasn't true. Maybe the reporter picked up on it before then."

Jana leaned back against the seat and expelled a long breath. "I'm glad this evening is over. My face is stiff from smiling so much." She lifted a hand and rubbed it against her cheeks.

"You were beautiful tonight," Miles said unexpectedly. "And you were great with the reporters. Precious heart, I believe you're going to make a perfect politician's wife. You say and do exactly the right thing at the right time."

"Only until election day," she reminded him.

"After that I'll be returning to a private life of my own—and when I do, I may take a solemn vow never to smile again."

"That would be a shame," Miles said lightly. "A terrible shame."

Jana was unsure whether he meant her vow to never smile again or her leaving him, but she did not have the nerve to ask.

They had arrived home only long enough for Jana to shed her jacket and heels and for Miles to put the kettle on in the kitchen for hot tea when the telephone rang. Jana shuffled in stockinged feet across the room to answer it. To her amazement, it was Allen Montgomery.

"I'll be in Charleston tomorrow on business," he told her, "and I was wondering if I could see you."

"Of course," Jana replied. "Come for lunch. It'll be wonderful to see you."

Miles had returned with her cup of tea, and there were scowl marks slashing the skin between his eyebrows as he listened to her side of the conversation. Jana tensed beneath the scrutiny, and then she was suddenly angry. Miles didn't mind hurting her with his attentions to Edie, so why should she care about his disapproval now? Besides, it helped her pride somehow, having him realize that she was attractive to another man.

With deliberation she forced herself to laugh in what she hoped was a lighthearted, flirtatious way as she added, "Fine, Allen. I've missed you, too. I'll look forward to tomorrow."

"A boyfriend, obviously," Miles stated after she had hung up the receiver.

"That's right," she said in a cool voice that hid her nervousness about the black expression on his face. "From Atlanta. He's coming for lunch tomorrow."

"Perhaps you ought to invite him to stay for dinner, too," Miles growled beneath his breath, "because otherwise you'll be eating alone!"

He turned on his heel and went out of the house, leaving Jana to stare after him in absolute shock.

Chapter Five

By eleven o'clock the next morning, Jana was as frantic as a nervous cat. Daisy found her, still in her nightgown and negligee, pacing the living room.

"I did like you said, Mrs. Parrish, and made a shrimp salad, rolls, and that ham casserole you wanted. The table is set, if you'd like to check it. Also, you didn't put a centerpiece on the table yet." Her piercing gaze was critical as she eyed Jana's attire. "Are you going to receive your guest dressed like *that*?"

Jana glanced down at herself, only that instant realizing that she still needed to dress before Allen arrived. She grimaced. "Of course not," she answered the maid. "I was about to go upstairs and get ready. I'm just running late today." She made a supreme effort to sound casual and normal. "My friend isn't supposed to arrive until noon, but just in case he decides to show up early, I'd better go dress now. Would you be an angel, Daisy, and do the centerpiece yourself? Some of the azaleas from the backyard, perhaps?"

"I'll take care of it, Mrs. Parrish," Daisy assured her in a placid voice. "You didn't say, but is Mr. Parrish planning to be here, too?"

"No!" Jana's voice came out with a razor-sharp edge, and she bit her lip in frustration because of it. "No," she tried again in a calmer tone, "I'm afraid he won't be able to make it. He's very busy at the office today."

"That's too bad." Clearly, Daisy disapproved of men visiting married ladies while their husbands were absent.

"Yes, isn't it?" Jana replied as pleasantly as she could manage. "All right, Daisy. It seems you have everything well in hand, so I'll go upstairs now."

She climbed the stairs slowly. Every muscle in her body complained of fatigue. It was a wonder she wasn't black and blue from tossing in the bed all night.

Damn Miles anyway! she thought with swift fury mingled with agonizing worry. Where was he? He had no right to put her through all this anxiety just because Allen was coming. After all, it wasn't as though he had always been a model husband, so what right did he have to play an outraged one?

She went into the bathroom and stripped off her clothing and stepped into the shower. Her aching limbs would have greatly benefited from a nice, long soak in the tub, but there was not enough time for that, not with Allen coming in a short while.

Today she wished she had never even heard of Allen Montgomery. Her little prideful plan of last night had gone sadly awry. All she had wanted was to prove to Miles that she could interest other men, not to drive him completely from home!

Yet that was exactly what had happened. Absently, Jana rubbed soap over her breasts, stomach, and thighs. Miles had not come back last night after storming so furiously from the house, and he had not come home this morning either.

But what really frightened her was that he had also not appeared at the office today. Vigorously, she rubbed the washcloth up and down her arms and legs, washing away the soap film. But it was not possible to scrub away her fearful thoughts. She had called the office to see if he was all right—ready, even, to apologize to him for inviting Allen to lunch without consulting with him first. But Kathleen, his secretary, said he had not arrived.

That had been awkward, she mused as she allowed the water to play across her shoulders and back. She had had to think quickly to cover up her error in calling. Improvising, she had told the secretary that she suddenly remembered after all that Miles had mentioned having an early meeting. She could only hope that Kathleen had bought the story and that she had not created an uncomfortable situation for Miles whenever he did finally return to the office.

Only, where was he? The question gnawed at her as she turned off the taps, stepped out of the shower, and dried herself.

Back in the bedroom, she dressed with the greatest lack of enthusiasm. As worried and upset as she was over Miles, she did not see how she was going to be able to entertain Allen. If she only knew where to reach him, she would call and cancel the whole thing. But unfortunately she had not thought to ask such a question last night.

At last she was ready in a mauve-colored dress with a simple fitted bodice, short sleeves, and a skirt that swirled from her hips. A glimpse of herself in the mirror as she reached for her perfume on the dresser told her the dress was a mistake. Today she was far too pale and wan. She should have worn something more colorful. But it was too late to do anything about it now. From her opened door she heard the doorbell ringing downstairs and Daisy's footsteps as she went to answer it.

With grim determination Jana arranged a smile on her lips and left the room. Somehow she would get through this lunch, and somehow she would manage to keep her anxious thoughts at bay. The last thing she wanted was for Allen to guess that anything was wrong.

"Jana!" Allen came forward eagerly to meet her when she entered the living room. He gripped both her hands and, leaning forward, kissed her cheek. "You're more beautiful than ever, my dear!"

"Thank you." Nervously, she withdrew her hands from his. "Have a seat, Allen," she invited as she seated herself in the safety of a chair rather than on the sofa. "You're looking marvelous yourself. How have you been?"

Allen sat down on the sofa at the end nearest her chair and gazed at her with open admiration. "I'm fine," he answered. "And you?"

She nodded, but then she averted her eyes from his keenly assessing gaze. He was studying her intently, as though by sheer willpower he would be able to read her thoughts. "Tell me," she suggested lightly, "how are things at the office?"

Allen leaned back against the cushions in a relaxed manner, apparently taking her hint to keep the conversation on an impersonal plane. "About the same," he replied. "Megan got married, and John is getting a divorce."

Office gossip might have been a safe topic, but Jana winced inwardly at the word *divorce*. She wondered bleakly if she might be involved in the same process very soon.

Daisy came to announce lunch, and with relief Jana got to her feet and led the way into the dining room. Throughout the meal they stuck to safe topics, and she began to think perhaps she would be able to get through this meeting without too much difficulty after all.

Occasionally she stole a glance at Allen. He was dressed casually in tan slacks, an open-necked tan-and-white-striped knit shirt, and a brown blazer. He was better-looking than she had remembered. His smile came easily. His hazel eyes often twinkled at her as he teasingly attempted to convince her that the office could no longer manage without her and that she must return. But though Allen was very masculinely appealing, Jana felt not the slightest flutter. Even though things between herself and Miles were at a dreadful pass, she knew that at least she had done the right thing by putting an end to Allen's hopes concerning her. She could never have made him happy if she had married him, because she could never love him. In deep despair, she realized that, in truth, she would never be able to love any man except Miles. Her heart had always been entirely possessed by him, whether he desired it or not.

Daisy brought their dessert and coffee, and after she left them alone again, Allen dropped his casual demeanor. "I've missed you, Jana," he said huskily. "Terribly."

"Please don't," she begged. "It's no good, and—"

"Are you happy?" He cut off her words with his own and leaned forward, peering deeply into her eyes. "You came back to him, but is it what you want?"

Again Jana's pride rose to the surface. She would

rather have died than admit how things really were. She summoned up a dazzling smile and nodded. "I'm very happy," she said with assurance. "Miles and I are completely reconciled. To tell the truth, I've never been happier. I'm in love with my husband," she added firmly for good measure, "and he's in love with me."

"Truer words were never spoken."

With a start, both Jana and Allen turned toward the voice from the doorway. There stood Miles, with a charming smile on his face.

Jana stared wordlessly. He had obviously been in the house for some time; his hair glistened, still damp from a shower, his face was freshly shaven, and he was neatly dressed in a pair of casual blue slacks and a white golf shirt instead of the suit he had been wearing when he left last night.

Indolently, as though he had all day, he came across the room and paused at Jana's side. He bent and kissed her forehead. "Sorry I missed lunch, precious heart," he said lightly, "but I just couldn't get away from those meetings any earlier. But I'm off for the rest of the day." Now he straightened, turned to Allen, and offered his hand. "You must be Allen Montgomery," he said with urbane smoothness. "I'm Miles Parrish, Jana's husband. I'm sorry I wasn't able to be here when you arrived as I had planned, but I'm sure my *wife* was able to adequately entertain you." There was only the softest emphasis on the word *wife*, but it was there, all the same.

Allen rose from his chair to accept Miles's handshake. "It's nice to meet you," he responded politely, but there was a wary, uneasy expression on his face.

Miles waved him back into his chair. "Sit down and finish your dessert, Allen," he said hospitably as he went around the table and sat down himself. He flashed a smile at Jana, who was still staring numbly at him, as though he were a ghost.

At last she found her tongue. "Have you eaten?" she asked. "I'll go tell Daisy to bring you a plate."

"Never mind," Miles told her. "I've already snatched a bite, and Daisy is going to bring me some coffee."

On the heels of his words Daisy arrived with a cup of coffee for Miles and a slice of cake to go with it.

"Well," Miles said heartily after he had sipped at his scalding coffee, "have you two been having a nice visit?"

"Yes, we have." Allen seemed to have recovered composure before Jana had. "You have a lovely home here, Mr. Parrish."

"Thanks. But do call me Miles," Miles said with a smile. "Any friend of Jana's is a friend of mine." Now he turned the full force of his smile upon her. "Darling, have you shown Allen your collection?" He indicated the case near the window.

"There hasn't been time yet," Jana replied. "Allen, would you like more coffee?"

"No, thanks," Allen answered. "The meal was delicious. Too bad you missed it, Miles."

Miles nodded agreeably. "How long are you going to be in town?" he inquired in a casual voice.

"Only today. I've got a business meeting this afternoon and then an evening flight back home."

"Too bad. If you were going to be here longer, Jana and I could show you the sights. Or do you already know Charleston?"

Allen shook his head. "No. This is my first trip."

"Then you must come back when you have more time. There's a lot of history in this area, if you like that sort of thing."

For the next hour there was only genial conversation in the same vein—mostly between the two men. After their dessert they had returned to the living room. Miles, with an arm draped lightly across Jana's shoulders, had pulled her down onto the sofa close beside him while Allen was left to take a nearby chair.

Jana resented the possessive way Miles was behaving. His arm, stretched along the back of the sofa behind her, would occasionally stray to her shoulders, or his hand would give a playful tweak to her hair that brushed against his arm. But what she most resented was the endearing way he addressed her and smiled at her, just as though they were indeed a happily married couple. She was well aware that he was acting this way because he must have overheard her telling Allen that they loved each other; but, really, he was carrying this charade too far! Every time he spoke to her, it was "sweetheart" this or "darling" that or "precious heart" something else. Jana felt like screaming, and it took every ounce of self-control that she had to keep still and sit there smiling as though she were enjoying it all.

She was reaching the breaking point when Allen finally took his leave. The instant he was gone, she turned on Miles like a shrew. "Why did you have to spread it on so thick?" she demanded. "Now he's bound to be suspicious! *Nobody* can possibly be that happy together!"

Miles only laughed at her. "If I overdid it, so did you. You burrowed up to me like a child to its teddy bear."

"I did not!" she denied hotly. "You made me sit that close to you, and you know it! It would have created a scene if I had tried to move away!"

"If I recall correctly," Miles taunted, "when I first arrived, you were the one who was so earnestly trying to convince him of how much in love we are."

"Well, how was I to know you'd be there standing eavesdropping?" she snapped angrily.

Miles chuckled, the sound rumbling from deep within his chest. "Oh, it's all right for you to put on a little act, but not me?" He shrugged. "I was merely trying to help you out."

"I don't need your help!" she flared.

"Why were you feeding him such a line, anyway?" Miles asked curiously. "Last night I was under the distinct impression that you cared for him, and it was quite obvious today that he's in love with you."

Jana turned away from him, and all at once her shoulders drooped like wet feathers. "I don't know." She sighed. "It just seemed the right thing to do. For one thing, I don't want anyone's pity. For another, there's no sense in allowing Allen to continue thinking there can ever be anything between us. It would be unrealistic to ask him to wait until you and I are finally free."

"That makes sense," Miles said cheerfully, "especially since there's some question about whether you will ever be free to marry again."

Jana whirled around to face him. "What do you mean? Of course I will . . . right after the election next year."

"We'll see." His tone was maddeningly mild. "Right now I want you to go pack us a weekend bag. I called Kathleen and told her I wouldn't be back to the office until Monday—and, Mrs. Parrish, you and I are going to Hilton Head."

Jana's heart lurched. "And why," she asked unsteadily, "would we want to go there?"

"Why did we ever go there?" Miles countered.

To make love, she thought wildly, but she could not bring herself to say the words. She merely gazed at him, almost in a state of shock that he had even suggested it . . . especially after last night.

Miles glanced quickly at his watch. "You've got exactly a half hour," he stated with crisp decision. "While you're packing I'll call the office about a couple of things I forgot to tell Kathleen earlier. Then I'll let Mom know we'll be out of town for a few days." When he looked up and saw her still standing there, he ordered gruffly, "Get a move on, woman! We've got a drive ahead of us."

One hour later they were headed south toward Hilton Head Island, a resort that appealed to sports lovers of many types. It boasted tennis courts that attracted pros to championship tournaments, and it also had many excellent golf courses, a marina for boats, lovely beaches, and even historic forts that had been occupied during the Civil War by Union forces.

Jana looked forward to the weekend with mixed emotions. It would be wonderful to see the island again and to enjoy its many amenities. She had always loved to go there and relax. But the memories the place conjured up in her mind were perhaps better left in the past.

So why, she wondered, darting a quick sideways glance at Miles, did he want to take her there now? Last night he had been so furious that he had walked out on her; today he acted cheerful and happy and had pretended to be madly in love with her in front of Allen. But pretense was one thing, reality another, and Jana couldn't help but think that coming to Hilton Head now was a mistake.

Miles had already owned a condominium there when they were married, and that was where they had gone for their honeymoon. They had spent wonderful golden days on the beaches, sailing in his boat that he kept at the marina there, golfing, and playing tennis. And making love. What magic nights they had spent there together, not only during their honeymoon but on their frequent weekend trips as well.

By the time they arrived it was late afternoon, and they were both glad to be able to leave the confines of the car and flex cramped muscles. The bright, cheery colors of the living room greeted Jana when they walked inside. In spite of her reservations about this trip, her spirits soared. Unlike their graceful old home in Charleston with its period furnishings, the condo was decorated with ultramodern pieces. The sofa was lemon yellow with white throw pillows. The tables were of chrome and glass, and there was a spacious, airy feeling about the room. An abstract painting done in bold yellows, oranges, and whites hung on one wall. Along the opposite wall were lemon-colored draperies that made a bright splash of color against the white interior. Not a single thing had changed since Jana had last been there, and for some reason that pleased her, though she did not attempt to analyze her feeling.

She went immediately across the room and pulled open the drapes. The wide windows provided an excellent view of the Atlantic Ocean. As she stood gazing out at the vivid expanse of blue water and paler blue sky meeting it she unconsciously let out a sigh of pure enjoyment.

"You always did love this place, didn't you?" Miles asked softly from just behind her.

"I suppose I did," she admitted, not taking her eyes off the view.

"We had some wonderful times here together." His voice was low and sensuously appealing. "Do you remember?"

"I prefer not to," she replied. Something thick was suddenly clogging her throat, and tears pricked at her eyes.

"That's strange," Miles said. "I, on the other

hand, never want to forget. Life offers so few joys that I want to preserve the memories of them very carefully."

Why was he doing this to her? Jana asked herself. Why was he torturing her so? She turned to him, and there was a grave look in his eyes instead of the teasing glint she had expected. It threw her off balance. For a long moment they simply gazed at each other as the strong emotions of the past held them bound together.

Then Jana gave a short, negative shake of her head. "Please," she pleaded brokenly, "please, Miles, don't. The past is over."

Slowly, he nodded. "Yes. And this is now." His mood changed swiftly and he smiled at her. "Let's have a drink to unwind before we go out to dinner."

They dined at their favorite seafood restaurant. Although the food was marvelous, as always, and the headwaiter, who had known them from the past, hovered over them with a beaming smile, Jana was scarcely impressed by either the food or the solicitous attention they received. Miles kept looking at her in such a way that it was difficult to concentrate on anything else. She knew she ate, smiled her thanks to the waiter, and somehow managed to get through the leisurely meal. But it was all done automatically rather than from any real awareness. She was only conscious of the man sitting opposite her, of the tender light in his eyes, of his soft-voiced conversation, of the gentle smile that played frequently over his lips. And it was all playing havoc with her intention of keeping a firm guard against memories of the past.

By the time they returned home, Jana's senses felt battered and bruised from her inner battle. She was keenly attuned to Miles's slightest movement, to the heady scent of his aftershave lotion.

The living room was softly lit by a single lamp in a corner. As Jana dropped her purse onto a table she tensed, knowing instinctively that Miles was watching her.

Nervously, she turned to face him, about to say good night, to go quickly to the guest bedroom and close the door firmly. But his gaze stopped her. Just as she had been earlier that day, she was helpless to look away, and the words she had been about to speak remained unuttered.

Miles broke the frozen spell by crossing the space between them. Jana knew he was about to take her into his arms and kiss her, and she was unable to prevent it.

When he did touch her at last, it was as though a dam had burst, drowning them both in the resulting flood. His arms pulled her fiercely against the lean, solid frame of his body and his mouth claimed hers, and Jana quivered as suppressed desire overtook her. Her arms went to his shoulders and one hand crept up his neck to muss his hair.

Miles's lips parted hers, and it was as though he were trying to devour her. The heat of their passion burned them both, and Jana, losing all control, pressed even closer to him in her need.

At last Miles raised his head, though he did not release her. His dark eyes were glazed by the emotions that held him. When he spoke, his voice was ragged and uneven. "No matter what our problems, precious heart, it's senseless for us to stay apart when we absolutely adore each other's bodies. I can't bear it and neither can you, so let's at least be honest about that."

Weakly, Jana nodded. She could not do otherwise while this fire raged through her, scorching her, consuming her. Her limbs were aching with unsatisfied longing. Though she knew she ought to put space between them so that she could think rationally and logically, she did not have the strength of will to do it.

Friday and Saturday were spun of magic, delicate cobwebs of joy and beauty and sunlight. Jana was aware that eventually the thread must break, that reality must intrude. But for those two exquisite days she thrust all but the present from her mind. It was as wonderful and special a time as their honeymoon had been. They played golf, idled away golden hours on Miles's sailboat, and walked hand in hand along the sandy beaches. And in between they made love . . . in the wee hours of the morning and again in the evening. They got up at three in the morning, starved, to cook frozen pizzas, and, in exhaustion, they would nap, wrapped close in each other's arms, in the late afternoon.

Jana was so happy it was almost frightening, and she knew that Miles felt the same. There was a relaxed, younger, almost boyish look on his face now. His eyes were always twinkling with a devilish amusement that lurked close to the surface. One morning he dunked her, fully clothed, in the bath because she had dared to taunt him about his less than marvelous golf score. And another time, when she had expressed a sudden craving for chocolate ice cream and he had teased her about her ravenous appetite these days, he had gone out to buy it for her and returned with not only ice cream but cookies, candy, peanuts, and chips and dip as well. Then he had insultingly extracted a single candy bar for himself and expressed the hope that the rest of the loot might tide her over until they returned home.

It seemed they were always laughing and joking,

always smiling, always touching each other. Jana wondered deep within herself whether things might not work out between them after all. When things were so perfect as this, it was easily believable. Delightful as the weekend was, however, not once did either of them speak of love, of their inner feelings. But to Jana it seemed as though she were always telling Miles of her love, because everything she did was silently proclaiming it.

On Sunday morning Miles surprised her and brought her breakfast in bed. On the tray was a small gift-wrapped package with a bright pink bow.

Jana, in her pale blue nightgown, was propped up against the pillows, totally unconscious of the alluring picture she made with her tousled hair and sleep-flushed face. She lifted a questioning glance to his face, and her heart leaped at the warm glitter in his eyes. And then, admiringly, her gaze slid downward. Miles wore only a white terry-cloth robe, and the bare expanse of his chest was visible at the open neckline. The tantalizing glimpse of his dark chest hair and his bronzed thighs protruding beneath the robe did crazy things to her senses.

He seemed oblivious of the destruction he was doing to her emotions. "Open the present," he instructed, reminding her of the tray on her lap.

Reluctantly, Jana dragged her gaze away from him and obeyed. And then she gasped aloud. Nestled inside the small jeweler's box was a beautiful ring of emeralds and diamonds. Next to her treasured engagement ring, it was the most gorgeous ring she had ever seen.

"It's magnificent," she whispered in an awed voice. "But . . . but why? It isn't Christmas and it's not my birthday." Again her gaze flew to his face.

A small smile softened Miles's lips. Yet there was also an odd sense of uncertainty about him that was startling for her to see in a man who was normally so confident in everything he said or did. "Now open the envelope," he said in a deep, husky voice.

Jana slit the envelope and pulled out the white card. It read, "Can we let the past go and make the rest of our lives as golden and happy as these days have been?"

"Are you . . ." Jana swallowed hard, then whispered, "Are you asking me to stay permanently?" Once more, she lifted her eyes to his face.

Miles nodded. The smile was gone and his dark gaze was somber as he asked, "Will you?"

"Yes," she whispered. Then she flashed him a brilliant smile. "Yes, Miles. It's what I want, too," she said in a rush of honesty.

"Wonderful girl!" Miles exclaimed, swooping down to kiss her. His action jarred the breakfast tray, spilling coffee over scrambled eggs and biscuits and strawberries. "Whoops!" he added as he realized what he had done. "At least it didn't spill in your lap. *That* might have sent you packing immediately!" They both laughed as he removed the tray of ruined food and placed it on the floor. Then he turned back to her, kissed her lips, and, lifting her hands with his, placed them around his neck. "I want to make love to you again right now, Mrs. Parrish," he said with soft urgency.

"And what about breakfast?" she teased.

"Woman, you're *always* hungry," he grumbled as his fingers slid the strap of her gown down to expose the soft, creamy mound of her breast. His lips played with hers, and then he murmured, "But maybe I can make you forget about food for a while."

"No question about it," she murmured back as her teeth nibbled at his lower lip.

They arrived back in Charleston with little time to spare before Dorothy's Sunday-afternoon dinner. She had insisted that the family get together today because Caroline and Bill would be there, their first visit since their wedding.

It was a lovely dinner. Dorothy, who enjoyed cooking these Sunday meals herself, had prepared a delicious roast and vegetable dishes and even home-made rolls. The conversation was animated and sparkling as Caroline and Bill, glowing with happiness, described their honeymoon trip to Niagara Falls. Fully at ease with each other for the first time in months, Jana and Miles were able to join whole-heartedly in the camaraderie of good company. Only one thing marred the perfection of the get-together; Guy had not come. It hurt Dorothy to see her family so split, and as she watched her mother-in-law trying to act completely happy, trying to hide her pain, Jana felt the stirrings of anger. Guy's anger toward Miles, justified or not, was no excuse to hurt his mother. Dorothy had done nothing to deserve such rude behavior from her son.

After the meal, the two girls insisted upon cleaning the kitchen. But though they scolded Dorothy and attempted to chase her out, she refused to be banished. In the end, the three of them did the chore.

"I can tell that you're miserable and that Bill beats you every day," Jana teased Caroline.

Caroline tossed her a sly grin. "True," she agreed, "but I figure I made my bed and now I have to lie in it."

"Girls!" Dorothy exclaimed in a scandalized voice. "Such talk!" But she was smiling. "It's appar-

ent to any idiot how happy Caroline is," she added.
Then her studious gaze was on Jana's face. "But it
seems to me there's also a sort of glow about you
and Miles today. Do I dare to pin any hopes on
that?"

Jana felt her face redden beneath her mother-in-
law's intent scrutiny, and she hesitated before answering. What if, somehow, things didn't work out
this time after all? But then she glanced down at her
right hand and saw the ring Miles had given her only
this morning. Remembering the reason, she felt
suddenly exuberant. She smiled at Dorothy and
nodded. "I think so," she said softly. "We just had
the most wonderful weekend together."

"Thank God!" Dorothy said fervently. "Maybe
we'll get this family straightened out yet!"

The following day, Jana decided to attempt some
straightening out herself. Miles would probably be
furious if he knew, so she said nothing of her plans to
him at breakfast.

After he was gone, she dressed simply in a navy-
blue suit with a red and white polka-dotted blouse.
The skirt felt a tiny bit more snug at the waistband
than usual, and she laughed at herself. The past
weekend she had been eating like a heavyweight
fighter, and Miles had enjoyed teasing her that all
that lovemaking was the cause of it. That, she
decided now, and pure happiness. All those months
they'd been apart and ever since she had returned,
she had only picked at her food like a sparrow, and
the result had been a too-thin body. Now, she
thought, perhaps her curves would fill out again to
their normal proportions.

When she arrived at Guy's law office, his secretary
was busy at the typewriter. As soon as she saw Jana
she paused and asked pleasantly, "May I help you?"

"I'd like to see Mr. Parrish, please, if he's free. I'm his sister-in-law, Jana Parrish."

"Please be seated," the girl said politely, rising from her desk. "I'll check and see."

Jana did not bother sitting down but instead glanced at the tasteful paintings on the walls. She especially liked the beach scene. It reminded her of the weekend just past.

The girl returned and smiled. "Mr. Parrish will see you now. This way, please."

When Jana entered Guy's private office, the secretary discreetly closed the door on them. Guy had risen from his chair behind the desk and was coming around to meet her.

"Jana!" he exclaimed. "What is it? Why are you here?"

Jana looked at him, so like Miles with his deep brown eyes and the shape of his head. The anger she had felt toward him melted. She smiled. "Can't I just drop in for a social visit?" she asked.

"You never have before," Guy pointed out bluntly.

"I came," she said, deciding to be equally blunt, "to see whether you're all right. You didn't appear at your mother's dinner yesterday, and she was very disappointed, very hurt."

A dark flush crept up from Guy's neck to his face. "I knew there would be company present that I didn't care to see."

Jana shook her head and sighed. "You're not hurting Miles's feelings nearly so much as you're hurting your mother, Guy. Don't you think it's time to end all these hostilities? No matter what else, Miles *is* still your brother, and you used to care for him a great deal."

"I idolized him," Guy admitted, "but now I know

what he's really like. Jana, how can *you* have forgiven what he's done?"

"I don't know that I have completely," she said honestly, "but I am trying. At first I tried for Dorothy's sake, but now I'm trying for my sake, and for Miles's as well. Listen to me, Guy. Several times Miles has said he's wanted to explain the truth to you and to me, but we've both refused to listen. Can it be possible that Edie might have been lying? Don't you think we both owe Miles at least the courtesy of letting him tell us his side of things? Before it completely tears the family into shreds?"

Guy walked over to the window and glanced out toward the harbor. "What good would that do, Jana?"

"What harm would it do?" she countered.

He was silent for a long time, so that for a while she believed he was not going to answer. But finally he turned and looked down at her with tortured eyes. "What do you want me to do?"

"Come to the house tonight and have a talk with Miles," she said quickly. "All I ask is that we both let him explain his side of the story. That's all."

At last Guy nodded. "I'll be there at seven."

"Thanks, Guy," Jana whispered. She went to him and brushed her lips against his cheek. "I'll see you tonight."

Jana called Miles at the office that afternoon and gave him a plausible story that she had to drive his mother somewhere that evening and would not be home until a little after seven. She wanted to give the two brothers a few minutes alone together before she arrived. She had a feeling it might be an easier meeting for them both if she were not present at first.

But when she did get home and went toward the front door, the door opened suddenly and Guy stormed out, slamming it behind him. When he saw Jana, he scowled darkly.

"I always thought you were my friend, Jana," he snapped.

Involuntarily, Jana took a step backward. "I was. I am," she stammered.

Guy gave an unamused laugh. "Then, if that's your idea of a joke," he said bitingly, jerking his thumb over his shoulder, pointing at the house, "it's not funny!" Without another word he stalked toward his car.

Completely bowled over by Guy's inexplicable anger, she climbed the steps to the porch and turned the doorknob. Then she walked inside to meet the scene that had so upset Guy.

Seated on the sofa were Miles and Edie. His arms were comfortingly around her shoulders as tears streamed down her face. It was like a very bad movie with a repeat of the same scene that had already been played earlier, Jana thought in stunned horror. The only difference was that this time it was set in the living room instead of the bedroom.

Chapter Six

The ugly little tableau swam before her blurred eyes. Jana's head felt suddenly light, and she swayed unsteadily. Again. It was happening all over again, and something inside of her shriveled up to die in that moment.

Unaware of what she was doing, she turned her head from side to side in agonizing little movements, as though her body would deny what she saw even though her mind must accept it. "No," she whispered beneath her breath. "Oh, no!"

She turned back toward the door, but her body moved in slow motion, like a robot. Now she was beyond thinking. Somewhere in the deep recesses of her mind, she realized that once again she was on the outside looking in and that she must go away.

She took one indecisive step before Miles's strong voice shouted compellingly, "No! Don't you dare walk out that door!" Only a split second later, his arms came around her, forcibly restraining her.

Her vision cleared as she gazed bleakly at him.
She was too weak, too numb, to even attempt to
fight him. Miles's face was as white as her own must
be, and a muscle twitched in his jaw. "You *will* not
run away from me again," he ordered. His hands
seemed to burn into her flesh as he held her. Then,
inexorably, he drew her away from the door and
back toward the other woman who still sat on the
sofa.

There was a hint of strain in Miles's voice as his
eyes bored deeply into hers once more. "Jana, I
swear to you it's not what it looked like." He gave
his head an abrupt shake. "I had no idea she was
coming, and I *still* have no idea why she did. She just
arrived at the door a few minutes ago, and as soon as
I invited her in she burst into hysterical tears. I was
only trying to calm her down so that she could tell
me what's wrong. You *have* to believe me!"

For an endless time they gazed searchingly at one
another, as though each were attempting to read the
other's mind. Miles's lips were pressed together into
a firm, hard line. But though his face looked like
chiseled, immobile marble, there was a desperate
sincerity in his eyes that she recognized.

At last Jana dragged her gaze from his and glanced
toward Edie. The other woman was dressed in a chic
pale aqua-blue dress that accented beautifully her
golden hair. But at the moment Edie looked far from
beautiful. Her shoulders drooped and tears streaked
her cheeks.

Even so, Jana's voice was hard as flint when she
spoke. She had recovered from the shock that had
temporarily rendered her so helpless and vulnerable.
Now a healthy anger warmed her blood.

"Why did you come, Edie?" she asked in a tone
that offered no sympathy for the weeping woman.

"Did you set up this scene for my benefit or for Guy's?"

Edie lifted tear-filmed blue eyes to Jana and cried, "I didn't set it up for . . . for anybody's bene . . . benefit." Her voice wobbled. "I came to . . . to talk to Miles and you be . . . because I'm so upset and worried. How was I to know Guy would come walk . . . walking through the door?" She buried her wet face in her trembling hands and began to sob with abandon.

In helpless frustration, Jana continued to eye her for a time with a cold lack of emotion. But the heaving shoulders, the agonizing sounds of sobbing that filled the room, began to weaken her anger. At last she threw a questioning glance to Miles.

He spread his hands out before him. "I told you," he said. "She's been like this ever since she arrived. I couldn't get any sense out of her. Do you suppose," he asked hopefully, "that you can calm her down and get her to talk?"

"Somebody has to," Jana said tartly. "Go fix her a drink, Miles. Something stiff." Squaring her shoulders with determined resolve, she went to the sofa and sat down beside the other girl, fumbled inside her own purse, which she still held, and pulled out a bunch of tissues. "Here," she said firmly, shoving them into Edie's hands, "dry your eyes and blow your nose. All this crying isn't helping anything, and until you stop we can't possibly help you."

The bracing, matter-of-fact tone of Jana's voice must have at last gotten through to Edie. After a moment she sniffed, shuddered, and then did as she was told.

"You've worked wonders," Miles said with a grim little smile as he handed the drink to Jana.

When Edie was done at last with mopping her eyes

and blowing her nose, Jana shoved the glass into her hand. "Take a couple of sips of that."

Edie swallowed some of the neat whiskey and gave another convulsive shudder. But, all the same, it seemed to help, because then she took a deep breath and appeared relatively calm, though her face was still swollen and splotched by tears. Jana felt a certain amount of surprise that Edie could possibly be reduced to looking so awful.

"Can you talk now?" Jana asked finally.

Edie nodded.

"Well," Miles said impatiently, "get going."

"Everything is just so awful," Edie answered at last. Fresh tears swelled in her eyes, and she dabbed them away with the damp, crumpled tissues. "Guy filed for divorce, you know. But even so, he's supposed to pay me maintenance support until it's final, and he hasn't done it. His secretary won't put me through to him at the office, and he won't answer his phone at his apartment. I've even tried writing him letters, but he won't answer them either. I don't . . ." She sniffled and stared down at her hands. "I don't know what to do, where to turn. I'm flat broke; I don't even have enough money to buy groceries, much less meet the mortgage payments or all the other bills. I can take Guy to court, of course. But even if I did, it would only take more time."

"Did you ever," Jana asked dryly, "think of getting a job and supporting yourself, Edie?"

Edie's watery eyes were suddenly trained on Jana. "Yes," she answered, surprising her. "But I'm not like you, Jana. I don't have training for anything. No one ever expected me to make it on my own in life, and now I don't know how!" Her voice grew shrill again. "If only Guy would help me out until I get on my feet, maybe take a business course or something. The house on the island would bring a good deal of money if I sold it. But I can't until the divorce settlement is final. And if I can't meet the payments on it, I'm going to lose it first!"

For the very first time, Jana felt a slight twinge of compassion for this girl who had caused so much damage, so much heartbreak, in all their lives. *At least,* she thought gratefully, *I had a Dorothy Parrish who saw to it that I was prepared to take charge of my own life.* Edie, the pampered socialite all her life, had been prepared for nothing.

Jana lifted her dark eyelashes and looked up at her husband. "We'll have to help her," she told him very quietly. "When all is said and done, Edie is still a Parrish and we can't allow her to go in need."

Miles nodded. "Of course." His gaze went to Edie. "We'll lend you the money you need for this month. In the meantime, try and see if someone can talk with Guy and get things straightened out."

"Thank you," Edie said unsteadily. One of her hands, which clung to Jana's, pressed tighter. "Thank you both. I don't know what I would have done if you . . ." At this point, she again burst into uncontrollable sobs.

Without stopping to think that this was a woman she detested, Jana gathered Edie into her arms, much as Miles had done earlier. As their eyes met above her head, they shared a wry smile of understanding.

"Help me get her upstairs to the guest room," Jana told him in an undertone. "She's far too hysterical to drive all the way back home tonight."

Together, each of them supporting her with their arms, they managed to get Edie up the stairs and into the bedroom. "Would you go get one of my nightgowns for her?" Jana asked Miles. "And bring a couple of aspirins and a glass of water, too. Maybe that will help to calm her."

"Do you have any tranquilizers?" Edie asked as she once again tried to catch her breath and speak rationally. "Mine are at home, and I really think I need one."

"I agree," Jana said softly as she turned back the covers on the bed. "But I've never taken them, so there aren't any in the house."

A half hour later, Jana left Edie tucked in bed, wearing her own green nightgown. But before she left, Edie held out a hand to her. "Thank you, Jana. For everything."

Downstairs, Miles waited for her. Tonight he had mixed their drinks. Jana accepted hers gratefully and sank down onto the sofa. Miles sat down beside her, and for a time they allowed blissful silence to descend upon them. After the stormy scene just past, they both felt a desperate need to let the tensions flow away.

At last Miles sighed and broke the peaceful quiet. "Somebody will have to talk to Guy. I'd do it, but I'm the last person on earth he would listen to. He wouldn't before, and he sure won't after tonight."

"That's true," Jana agreed, "and he wouldn't listen to me if I tried, either."

"Maybe he would." Miles turned to face her. "Guy always liked you."

Jana shrugged and took a sip of her drink. "Well, if he did before, he doesn't now. He thought I'd tricked him into coming here tonight."

"What are you talking about?" Miles asked as his eyes widened in amazement.

Jana recited what had happened that day. "I went to Guy's office and talked him into coming here tonight to see you, to finally listen to your explanation about Edie's claims. I thought if I could only bring the two of you together, alone, you could talk things out and clear them up." She shook her head.

"Only, Edie had to show up . . . of all times! And now Guy thinks I planned it as a joke of some sort!"

"Good God!" Miles exclaimed. "You mean you *asked* him to come so that I could tell him my side of the story?"

Wordlessly, she nodded.

"But . . . why?" he asked in confusion. "Since you would never allow me to explain anything to you either?"

"I don't know." Restlessly, Jana placed her drink on the lamp table and got up to prowl around the room. "Yes, I do, too. I did it for Dorothy. She was so upset yesterday when he didn't come for lunch that I just decided it was time for all this trouble to end."

Miles joined her where she stood beside the fireplace. "It wasn't because you'd begun to believe you'd been mistaken yourself about Edie and me?" he asked in a low, quiet voice.

"Oh, Miles, I don't know what to believe anymore!" Jana exclaimed. "I know what I saw that day, Edie with you in our bedroom, and I—" She broke off abruptly and turned away from him.

Miles's touch was gentle as his hands slid up and down her arms. "I have never slept with Edie in my life, Jana," he stated in a clear, measured tone. "Never."

Her shoulders twitched beneath his hands. "Never?" Her voice came out muffled and uncertain.

"Never."

"But . . . you were once engaged."

"Not even then," Miles said flatly. "Our engagement was never exactly a passionate affair." A tiny bit of amusement coated his voice. "Edie was far more in love with my money and the Parrish name than she ever was with me."

She turned to face him then, her eyes luminous
with the desire to believe. And yet doubts still
lingered. "But if that's true, Miles, then why did she
tell Guy you were having an affair?"

Miles shook his head, and his gaze was dark and
earnest. "God alone knows, except for Edie herself.
I've tried before to get it out of her. That day at the
wedding was one occasion," he said wryly, "when
you and Guy happened to see us talking. But she
refuses to give me any explanation. I suppose the
truth is she wanted out of her marriage and, in
anger, she made up a story she knew would be
certain to torture Guy. But you've got to believe me,
precious heart, I've never made love to Edie."

Jana stared at him for a long time, her eyes
searching for the truth. Miles's face was colorless
and even seemed to have a certain vulnerability as
he returned her gaze. Miles, *her* Miles, vulnerable
where she was concerned! It was a strange thing to
comprehend, because he had always been so self-
controlled, so self-sufficient, in absolute command of
his life and the situations that surrounded it. A law
unto himself. Yet tonight, with uncertainty and
anxiety clouding them, his eyes begged her to believe.

And, oddly enough, at last she did. And with
belief came a wild surge of joy. If she had been
mistaken about what she had seen that day, if Miles
truly had never had an affair with Edie, then surely it
must mean he had always loved her, Jana! It was an
exhilarating thought, and she could not hide her
happiness from him, because it glowed from her.

Her smile came, dazzling like a summer's morning
sun. "I believe you, Miles," she said.

He gathered her into his arms and crushed her
with a ruthless strength, of which they were both
oblivious, against his chest. "Oh, my darling, how

I've longed to hear you say that!" he whispered shakily. "It means so much to me to have your trust again. So very, very much." Slowly, he bent his head, and his mouth softened to possess the sweetness of hers.

The next morning was warm enough to breakfast outdoors in the walled garden behind the house. But the fine morning with its cloudless sky and the garden plants all bursting forth with tender spring leaves was scarcely noticed by either Miles or Jana.

"She's still asleep?" he asked.

She nodded. "Yes. I looked in on her a few minutes ago to see whether she wanted to come down and join us. I suppose she's still exhausted."

Miles frowned into the orange-juice glass he had just picked up. "When she does get up, write her a check for whatever amount she needs. In the meantime, we still haven't solved the problem of who's going to talk to Guy. Should we ask Mom?"

"I've been thinking about that," Jana replied, "and I believe it would just upset her more. She already knows Edie has had problems trying to get support from him. I think we ought to tell Caroline and have her call Guy."

"I think you're right," Miles answered. "If anybody can get through to him, she can. I'll call her as soon as I get to the office." Now he shook his head and smiled, dispelling the gloomy subject. "Are you all ready for your speech this afternoon?"

Jana grimaced. "Not very. I'd planned to study my notes last night, but, what with all the commotion, I never got around to it. I hope I don't do you more harm than good."

"That would be impossible." Miles's voice was incredibly warm, like the sun that beamed down upon their shoulders.

A few minutes later he left for the office. Jana sat
on at the table, delaying the chore of going inside to
study her speech notes. She had not admitted to
Miles how nervous she was about doing it, but dread
tightened the muscles in her neck in spite of the
soothing warmth of the sun.

She was just about to go inside when Edie joined
her, looking even worse than she had last night. Her
dress was crumpled, and her hair, though she had
obviously made an effort to brush it, looked wispy
and untidy. Her face was swollen and puffy from the
storm of tears the previous evening, and her eyes
were red-rimmed.

"Good morning," Jana said, forcing a bright
cheerfulness to her voice that she did not feel. "I
hope you rested well."

"Hardly at all," Edie said. "It must have been
near dawn before I finally fell asleep."

"That's too bad. Would you like some breakfast?
I'll get Daisy to make you some—"

Edie shook her head and interrupted. "No,
thanks. I'm not hungry."

"Coffee, then?"

Edie shook her head again. "I've got a queasy
stomach. Maybe just a glass of juice."

Jana went into the kitchen and poured the orange
juice herself since Daisy was busy with cleaning.
Then she returned to Edie, who sat, despondently
hunched, at the table.

"Here you are," Jana said, placing the juice on the
table and resuming her chair. She watched thoughtfully as Edie sipped at her drink. She was quite
obviously deeply unhappy, and Jana's natural compassion made her pity the woman. But she could not
help but think that Edie had brought her unhappiness down upon her own head.

Last night Miles had told her, sworn to her, that

he had never made love to Edie. She had believed
him then . . . *still* believed him. And yet there did
remain the tiniest seed of doubt. Miles had *not*
explained why Edie had told Guy they were having
an affair.

Jana shifted in her chair as the silence stretched. It
made no sense for Edie to tell her husband such a
dreadful thing if it wasn't true. It hardly made sense
even if it *were* true . . . unless she had counted on
marrying Miles after their respective divorces. But
last night, after that one instance when she had
found Miles holding Edie, neither of them had
appeared to have the slightest interest in the other.
Jana could not understand any of it, and for the first
time she wondered if it was possible that Edie was
mentally unbalanced.

She dismissed the notion at once. Edie might be
spoiled and pampered, she might be a liar and a
troublemaker, but she was not unbalanced. There
had always been a calculated shrewdness about her
that proved Edie knew exactly what she was doing at
all times. She was merely incomprehensible to others.

Now that they were alone together, Jana felt
tempted to ask straight out for an explanation. But
another glance at the woebegone face made her
hesitate. Edie's eyes were glistening with fresh tears,
though she was struggling to hold them back. Jana
could not bring herself to make matters worse.

"What's wrong?" she asked quietly. "Would you
like to talk about it?"

"Everything's wrong," came the quivering reply.
"Absolutely everything is wrong! Guy hates me so,
and I . . . I never wanted a divorce!"

Jana stared at her in disbelief, and now she did
voice the question that was uppermost in her mind.
"If you never wanted a divorce, why did you tell him

you were having an affair with Miles? I can hardly think of anything more certain to guarantee bringing about a divorce than a statement like that!"

"I won't talk about that!" Edie said on a rising note of hysteria. "I *can't* talk about that! You can't possibly understand my feelings . . . nobody does! Everyone thinks I'm so terrible, but *I'm* the one who's been hurt!" Tearfully, she jumped to her feet and rushed toward the house.

Numbly, Jana watched her go. Did Edie mean there *had* been an affair, then? That it was all true, after all, and that it was Miles who had let her down? And yet Edie had just said she had never wanted a divorce.

She shook her head, trying to clear it. She was not going to allow Edie's vague statements to upset her. That was like being on a seesaw, and she was tired of it. Briskly, Jana got to her feet and went toward the house. She had much to do today, and there was no more time to waste.

It was a hectic morning, coping with Edie's renewed bout of tears and trying to calm her into a state where it was safe for her to return to her own home. Then Jana had to make a mad rush for her own appointment at the hairdresser's. By the time she was seated beneath the hood of the dryer, Jana felt frazzled. She still needed to stop by the cleaner's to pick up the dress she would wear that afternoon. But at least the enforced time beneath the dryer gave her a chance to rehearse her notes.

In spite of her fears, the speech went well. Jana had all but memorized it and scarcely needed to glance at the index cards in front of her. Also, she was acquainted with a number of the ladies who were present, since Dorothy Parrish was also a member of the club. They had all greeted her so warmly when she arrived that somehow her nervousness had simply disappeared.

"You were wonderful, Jana," her mother-in-law beamed afterward. "I was so proud of you!"

"Thanks." Jana grinned. "All the same, I hope there won't be many occasions like this in the future. I'd much rather let Miles do his own talking."

But apparently her talking wasn't done. She had barely gotten back home when the telephone rang. It was a reporter wanting to do a profile on her for a newspaper article that would appear in a number of papers throughout the state. Sighing with exasperation, Jana assented to do the interview, but that evening she complained bitterly to Miles.

They were in bed, each propped up against mounds of pillows. Miles supposedly was watching a television program, while Jana had an opened book in her lap. "Why should anyone be interested in me, anyway?" she demanded of him. "You're the one who will be running for office."

Miles grinned. "People like to know a little of the personal side of the lives of their potential politicians, but lately it *does* seem like you're getting more attention than I am. Maybe you should run for Congress instead of me."

For an answer, Jana snatched up one of the pillows, whacked Miles on the head with it, and then, giggling, tried to make her escape.

She got one foot on the floor as he grabbed at her other leg and pulled her back across the bed. "Want to fight, do you?" he growled from low in his throat. "I'll teach you a lesson you'll never forget!" He pulled her roughly into his arms, imprisoning her so that she could not get away, and almost smothered her with his kisses. An instant more and they had both forgotten politics, publicity, and family problems. There were only the two of them in their own special universe.

The next morning, Jana awoke and stretched luxuriously beneath the covers. A glance at the clock told her she had overslept again . . . something she had been prone to do of late, for no accountable reason. Miles's side of the bed was empty and cool, telling her he had risen much earlier. By now he was bound to already be behind his desk, and once again he had had to prepare his own breakfast. She felt guilty about that, but not *too* guilty, since it was as much his fault as hers. If he had awakened her, she would willingly have gotten up to do it herself.

Lately things had been wonderful between them, in spite of the one bad evening when Guy and Edie had both arrived. Miles had done what he could about that situation. Last night he had told her he had talked with Caroline and she had promised to call Guy. But what the outcome was Jana did not know, and today she really did not much care. She felt happy, and the day ahead was hers to do with as she pleased. Daisy would not be coming today, and Jana planned to enjoy her own kitchen by baking a pie, maybe a cake as well. She wanted to prepare a super meal for Miles in the evening to make up for the lack of breakfast.

She got up and went into the bathroom to take her shower, but her thoughts dwelled tenderly on her husband. It was incredible how close they had become lately. It was so like the way their marriage had been in the beginning. Every evening Miles discussed his business problems with her, sometimes asking for her opinion, sometimes merely using her as a sounding board for his ideas and thoughts. They often went out together, too, to dinner or a movie, or an occasional party. For the coming weekend, if the weather was fine, they had plans to play golf.

Miles seemed not to want to exclude her from even the smallest facet of his life, and Jana could not help but be pleased that he always wanted her with him.

And yet there was still a little reserve between them. They didn't acknowledge it, didn't speak of it, but it was there all the same. They had never entirely cleared up the matter of Edie. Once, when Jana happened to mention Allen, only in connection with the job she had held with him, Miles's mood had swiftly altered from mellow good humor to black brooding. They were one again in their marriage in every way, physical and mental, with perfect rapport, except for their deepest, most intimate emotions. But it was as though they were both fearful to touch that part of their innermost beings lest they open a Pandora's box and learn things neither of them wanted to know. Miles did not vow his love again, and Jana kept a careful guard over her own secret feelings. He obviously wanted their marriage to succeed this time. But it would be horrible, unthinkably dreadful, if she ever accidentally allowed him to realize the depths of her love for him and he could not honestly tell her he felt the same way.

An hour later such disturbing thoughts had been banished from her mind. Jana ate a hearty breakfast while she studied recipes and was soon engrossed in rolling out pie dough and preparing peaches for the filling. Peach pie was one of Miles's favorites, and she hummed to herself as she worked.

When it was ready, she slid it gently into the oven and then sat down with her second cup of coffee for the day and went through cake recipes. A year ago she had learned to bake a fancy specialty cake, with chocolate pudding as a filling and sprinkled on top with pecans. But today she really wanted something different and not quite so complicated. Perhaps, she thought as she flipped a page in her cookbook, a carrot cake. She had never tried one of those before.

She was studying the list of ingredients to determine whether she had on hand everything that was necessary when the telephone interrupted her concentration.

It was probably Miles, she thought with a faint smile on her lips as she crossed the room to pick up the receiver from the wall telephone. He was probably all set to tease her about sleeping so late!

But it was not Miles, it was his mother, and Jana sensed at once that something was wrong by the odd sound of her voice.

"Are you busy?" Dorothy asked.

"Sort of. I'm baking Miles a peach pie."

"Oh." There was a long pause, then: "When will you be done?"

Jana glanced at the clock. "In about forty minutes or so. Why?"

"Could you come over here when you're through? I need you, Jana." Her voice was unsteady and frankly pleading.

Alert and tense now, Jana said, "Certainly. What's wrong? Are you ill? If so, I'll come now."

"No, no, go ahead and finish your baking," Dorothy said. "I'm all right. It's Edie."

"Edie?" Jana asked blankly.

"Yes, she's here now, and there seems to be a very big problem. So will you come when you can?"

"Of course. Dorothy, do you want me to call Miles?" Jana suggested. "If it's important, I'm sure he would—"

"No!" Dorothy exclaimed with a sharp edge of panic. "I don't want him here! Not yet!"

"All right." Jana sighed, a bit impatient now with Dorothy's strange secretiveness. "I'll be there in about an hour."

Her pleasure in the day vanished as she hung up the telephone. Edie again! It seemed the girl knew how to do nothing but upset other people's lives! And what could be the problem today? she wondered. Only a couple of days ago they had given her enough money to get by for at least a month. Surely even Edie hadn't run through it all already!

Jana chewed her lip irritably as she went to peep inside the oven. If that was the case, she was going to sit Edie down and give her a lecture she would never forget! It wasn't as though either Miles or Dorothy couldn't afford to help her out with money, but it was the principle of the thing. Everybody these days needed to learn to live within the framework of a budget and Edie was no exception.

She had to shelve the idea of the cake. So, while the pie finished baking, Jana went back upstairs to change from her faded jeans and sloppy T-shirt into neat, creamy yellow slacks with a yellow- and brown-printed blouse.

Threatening rain clouds passed overhead as Jana drove the short distance between her house and Dorothy's. There would probably be a heavy shower before the afternoon was over. The dark clouds cast a grayish color over the harbor, so that the water looked dull and uninviting.

When she arrived, as usual Jana did not bother ringing the doorbell but simply opened the door and walked inside. From the living room she could hear the low murmur of voices.

When she stepped into the room, she saw that Edie sat in a chair, presenting a duplicate of the picture she had given a few evenings ago. Her face was swollen and blotched, her eyes red, and tears trickled down her cheeks.

Jana glanced sharply toward Dorothy, who stood proudly erect before the fireplace. She was wearing a simple blue dress that cast bluish highlights on her gray hair, and her face was a mask of self-control. Only her hands betrayed her, for they were trembling.

"What's wrong?" Jana asked bluntly.

Dorothy Parrish sucked in a deep, shuddering breath. "Edie," she said with careful precision, "is pregnant."

Chapter Seven

The room whirled and spun like a crazy meteorite tumbling haplessly through space. Before her eyes, colors jumbled and ran together, interspersed with sparkling flashes of light. Jana's stomach heaved and flipped over as well, and a numbing weakness attacked her limbs. There was a loud buzzing noise filling her ears, blocking out all other sounds. For a moment she thought she might faint, welcomed the notion, even, for then oblivion would come, a wonderful black pit of emptiness, of nothingness.

"Are you all right? Jana, what *is* the matter with you?"

From far away came Dorothy's voice. Jana knew she must rouse herself, must be lucid and coherent, must hide something. Yes, but what was it? She squeezed her eyes shut to block out the blurred whirlwind of the spinning room. Gradually the screaming noise in her ears receded; slowly, the sickness in her stomach faded. When she dared to open her eyes again, the room had reverted to normal.

She became aware that Dorothy was holding her wrist and peering intently into her face. "What is it?" Dorothy asked in a commanding voice. "What's wrong with you?"

Dully, Jana gazed at her and shook her head. "Nothing. I'm fine. I guess I was just stunned by your news."

Dorothy grimaced. "No more than I was, I can assure you. Come sit down, my dear, and I'll pour you a cup of hot tea."

Weakly, Jana allowed herself to be led to the sofa, where she sank down, grateful that she could get off her unsteady legs. A tea tray was on the table before her, and Dorothy busied herself pouring out a cup and liberally dosing it with sugar before handing it to Jana.

After she had taken a sip of the scalding, too-sweet drink, Jana felt the color rushing back to her face. Then she turned at last toward the young woman in the chair adjacent to her and said harshly, "Oh, Edie, do stop crying! It just won't solve anything!"

Surprisingly, Edie did stop. She glared at Jana sullenly. "You'd be crying, too, if you found yourself in the position I'm in, with no husband to support you."

"No, I wouldn't," Jana denied. "I'd be far too busy trying to figure out what to do next."

"But I don't *know* what to do!" Edie cried out in despair.

Jana gazed thoughtfully at her for a long moment. She shouldn't be so hard on Edie, she supposed. The girl obviously lived on her emotions all the time, feeling rather than thinking. Jana knew Edie couldn't possibly *enjoy* all that crying. So it was going to be up to Dorothy and herself to help. She tried to swallow down the feeling of nausea that knowledge gave her.

"How far along are you?" she asked bluntly.

"About five months."

Jana's softly winged eyebrows flew upward in astonishment. "So long? Why have you kept it a secret until now?"

"Because"—tears glistened in Edie's eyes once more—"by the time I knew for certain, there was already all the trouble between Guy and me. I knew if I told him, he would only hate me more than he does already!" Her lips trembled, and she lowered her head in an effort to hide it.

"Edie is going to move in here with me until after the baby is born," Dorothy said. "She told me how she had to borrow money from you and Miles, and she's obviously not going to be in any condition to look for employment for months to come. So there's no point in her continuing to struggle like this. Also, I don't want her living out on the island alone in that house. What if she got ill or fell or something and no one was there to care for her? So she's going to stay here where I can look after her properly."

Jana nodded. "I think that's a good idea," she agreed quietly. "She certainly shouldn't be left all alone during her last months of pregnancy. If you want me to, Edie," she added, "I'll go with you out to the house and help you pack."

"Thanks." Edie sniffed and wiped away a tear. "But Dorothy's going to take me this afternoon."

"There's one thing," Jana said. "Guy has to be told . . . and at once."

"Why?" Edie's mouth turned down in a pout. "I don't want him to know. He'll just blow up again and—"

"It doesn't matter how he reacts," Jana said

firmly. "He has to know, because he will have to
drop the divorce suit. He cannot go ahead with the
divorce while you're carrying a child. He'll have to
postpone it."

"I've already thought of that," Dorothy said,
"and you're right, Jana. Guy has to be told, and the
sooner the better. If Caroline were still living here,
I'd ask her to do it. But since she isn't, you'll have to
tell him instead."

"Why me?" Resentment coated Jana's voice.
"Why can't you do it?"

Dorothy shook her head. "My son is going to be
angry enough with me when he learns that Edie will
be living in my house. He's going to feel I'm
betraying him, but I have no choice. Edie is carrying
my grandchild, and that is more important than
personal differences or desires on the part of any of
us. Do you understand me, Jana?" Her blue eyes
were piercing as she gazed at her; silently, they
spoke far more than her mere words had done. "The
baby's welfare must be the only consideration now,
no matter what happens or who gets hurt."

"Yes." Jana looked down at her clasped hands.
"Yes, Dorothy, I do understand."

Silently, Dorothy reached out and covered Jana's
hand with hers. It was meant to be a loving, comfort-
ing gesture, but Jana was beyond comfort, beyond
Dorothy's gentle love. Her entire world had once
more shattered like a broken window, and she
shuddered from the winter chills that, unhampered
by a protective glass pane, crept into her heart.

She glanced toward Edie again, and Edie looked
back guilelessly. How, Jana wondered bitterly, could
she sit there looking so innocent after dropping her
latest atom bomb upon the Parrish family? A surge
of white-hot anger raced through her, but as quickly

as it arose, it faded. Hating Edie was not the answer and doing so would help no one, including herself.

Even so, Jana could no longer look at her. The sight of Edie brought her such raw pain that she ached all over as though she had a virus. She knew she could not stay in the house another minute. Quickly, she got to her feet and somehow mustered a smile for Dorothy's sake. "I'll speak to Guy soon, I promise. But right now I must go." Without waiting to see whether her mother-in-law might have anything further to say, she hurriedly left the room.

The last place Jana wanted to go when she left Dorothy's was back to her own house. But as she went outside to her car raindrops spattered her head. With her emotions in such a chaotic state, she knew she was in no shape to be driving around, even if the sky weren't so threatening.

When she returned home, the silence was overwhelming, the rooms gloomy and dark. But Jana did not turn on the lights. In the kitchen she gazed scornfully at the pie she had so happily prepared a few hours ago. She laughed aloud; the sound was eerie, almost frightening, in the oppressive quiet, echoing against the walls, taunting, derisive.

Abruptly, she turned to the window and gazed out at the sodden garden. *I must stay calm,* she told herself. *I cannot fall to pieces over this. I will not cry the way Edie does!*

She buried her face in her hands and fought back the scalding tears. What was she going to do? Dear God, she wondered frantically, what *was* she going to do?

Everything was crystal clear now. It always had been, but, fool that she was, she had allowed Miles to persuade her to believe otherwise.

Edie was going to have Miles's child! Unbearable

as it was, she had no choice but to face reality. Miles had lied when he had sworn there had never been anything between him and Edie! And how easily Jana had been convinced, because she had wanted so desperately to believe him.

Now she understood so many things. Such as why Edie had told Guy about the affair. She had had no choice, knowing as she must have that she was pregnant with Miles's baby! She had told her, Jana, only days ago that she had never wanted a divorce. But even Edie's sense of honor could not allow her to deceive her husband to the extent of letting him believe her child was his when in fact it belonged to his brother!

Jana lowered her hands, lifted her face, and stared out the window with burning eyes. That was probably the reason Edie had arrived so unexpectedly the other night. It hadn't been that she needed money at all! She had come to see Miles, to tell him her secret, but she had been unable to do so because of Guy's unexpected arrival and, only moments later, her own.

What good actors they were . . . Miles and Edie! They had behaved so indifferently toward each other that evening. Yet they had both carried inside their hearts the knowledge of their guilt, their unfaithfulness. And Edie had known as well that the results of their affair must soon be told.

And now . . . what to do? A chill of absolute despair crept up her spine. Jana shivered and rubbed her arms. Morally, Miles was responsible for Edie's child. If things were straightforward and simple, then they should both get divorces and marry each other as quickly as possible. Only nothing was straightforward; there was no easy solution.

Still hugging herself for warmth, Jana left the window and slowly made her way through the dark house, up the stairs, and into the spare bedroom. She hated to use the room again—Edie had slept here. But she had no choice. It was the only alternative to sharing Miles's bed, and she could no longer do that.

Without bothering to undress, she crawled into the bed and pulled the covers up to her neck, coveting what warmth they could provide, because by now she was trembling from head to toe.

And what about me? she asked herself now, at last facing the worst part of all. *What am I going to do? How am I going to manage?* The question haunted her, and for the first time a wayward tear strayed down her cheek.

It was not official yet, it was still unconfirmed by a qualified doctor, but Jana knew. She, too, was pregnant. Lately there had been too many signs, almost infallible signs. Though she had not suffered from morning sickness as many women did, she knew with certainty that the increase in her appetite, the bloom in her cheeks, and that odd, unfathomable, but utterly-to-be-trusted feminine instinct all meant only one thing.

It must have happened one of the first times they had made love after she had returned to Miles. Her more tightly fitting clothes testified it could not be more recent. And lately she had hugged the knowledge to herself with secret joy, a joy that had increased daily as she and Miles drew closer. Last night she had almost told him, but at the last moment had bitten back the words. Before she told him, she had wanted to have it verified by a doctor. Since her appointment at the clinic was not until the following week, she had decided to keep her secret just a little longer. But now the joy was gone. There was only this awful emptiness in its place.

She closed her eyes and tried to block out her

thoughts with sleep, but it would not come. She tossed and turned fitfully. The heavy rain shower had ended, and now bright sunlight flooded through the window, but its cheery promise did nothing to lift her heavy spirits.

The telephone rang, and the sudden jarring sound startled her. But Jana made no move to answer it. It might be Miles, and she did not want to speak with him, not yet. It was too soon; she must get herself pulled together first.

The ringing finally ended, and Jana sighed with relief. But it had roused her from her stupor. Here it was, early afternoon, and she was huddled in bed as though she were ill! Where was her spunk, her self-respect? she asked herself angrily. Was she going to start behaving like Edie, all teary-eyed and unable to take the least responsibility for her own life? Or was she going to get on with it? Just because people were desperately unhappy did not mean they had any right to curl up and become withered vegetables. She had always been too much of a fighter for that!

Resolutely, she flung back the covers, glanced down in distaste at her rumpled clothes, and went down the hall to her own room to change. She still had to see Guy; though she had never dreaded anything more, it had to be done. Better to get it over with now. And afterward, perhaps her head would be more clear, so that she could make a rational decision concerning her own life.

The rain-washed city had a fresh, clean smell to it as Jana drove toward Guy's office. Palmetto fronds glistened like emeralds. Oleander bushes proudly bloomed, paying homage to both the life-giving rain and the gentle warmth of the sun. It was as though all nature had just been reborn, and Jana wished she had been, too. But all she felt inside was dead.

Guy's secretary appeared startled to be confronted by her again so soon, and Jana smiled grimly to herself. It *did* seem that lately she was making a habit of visiting this office.

Guy was busy with a client, so Jana sat down and thumbed idly through yesterday's *Wall Street Journal.* But in spite of the alarming state of the economy, the headlines failed to command her undivided attention. Silently, she was rehearsing what she was going to say.

Guy came out himself to bid goodbye to his client, an elderly gentleman, and his dark eyes widened in surprise when he saw her. "Good-bye, Mr. White. I'll give you a call just as soon as the papers are drawn up," he said as he opened the outer door for the older man. As soon as it was closed, he whirled toward Jana. "What are you doing here?" His voice contained no hint of friendliness.

Jana shifted her eyes warningly in the direction of his secretary and said in an undertone, "Something's happened. I have to talk to you."

Guy stared at her as though he could read her mind, and then he sighed. "All right. Let's go into my office." As Jana rose and preceded him he added to his secretary, "Hold all calls."

As soon as they were behind his closed office door, he said sarcastically, "What is it, Jana? Do you want to invite me to pay another surprise visit to my brother? It wasn't a big enough laugh for you last time?"

"Don't!" Jana's voice broke, and, in a pleading gesture, she placed her hand on his arm. "Please, Guy, don't do this . . . to either of us. You know I didn't plan that. I was just as stunned to see Edie there as you were."

Guy jerked his arm away from her grasp. "Oh, of course!" he sneered. "That's why you got

Caroline onto me the next day about Edie's support."

Jana sucked in a ragged breath. "Do you mind if I sit down? What we've got to discuss is unpleasant, and I, at least, need the support of a chair."

"Be my guest." Guy waved an impatient hand toward a chair, but he continued to stand where he was, arms crossed, his thick eyebrows lowered in a frown, as Jana sat down. "If you're here on Edie's behalf about the money, you're wasting your time, just as I told Caroline. I don't owe a thing to my *wife*, and if she wants to take me to court over it, she's welcome. What I can't understand is how you can be on her side in all this!"

"It isn't a matter of being on sides," she answered slowly, "but Edie *is* a Parrish." Unshed tears rose up to clog her throat, making it impossible for her to speak for a moment. She dreaded with all her heart what she had come here to say, and she wondered how to start.

Suddenly Guy was beside her and his hand pressed down upon her shoulder. "Look, I'm sorry, Jana," he said contritely. "I shouldn't be shouting at you. I guess I know deep down that you didn't set me up that night." He removed his hand and went around the desk, dropping into his chair so that they were facing each other. "Now tell me," he added quietly, "why you came."

For an endless time Jana was silent. She stared at a plaque on the wall behind his left shoulder so that she would not have to meet his eyes.

"Edie has . . . moved in with your mother," she began gently.

"What?" Guy's voice was incredulous. "Don't tell me she's duped Mom into believing she's *that* desperate for help! Jana, I won't have it! She's not my mother's responsibility." He shifted in his chair and added crossly, "Oh, all right, I'll send her the blasted support money if it'll keep her out of Mom's hair!"

Jana shook her head. "The night you saw her at our house, Miles and I gave her money enough to get by on for a while. That's not the problem, Guy. It's far more serious than that."

Briefly, her eyes flickered across his face. There was puzzlement and confusion in his dark eyes, and she quickly glanced away again.

"Then," Guy prompted, "what is the problem?"

Jana sucked in a deep breath and plunged. "You must drop the divorce suit," she told him.

There was a startled silence, and then Guy asked in a low voice, "Have you gone crazy, Jana . . . or what?"

She shook her head. "Guy, I can't make this easy for you, so I'm just going to have to say this outright. Edie is pregnant."

This time the silence following her pronouncement was deafening. Jana tensed, waiting for the explosion that was bound to come.

But a full minute passed and there was no response. She forced herself to glance across the desk. Guy's face had turned a pasty white, and there was a stricken, sick expression glazing his eyes. Jana's heart lurched in sympathy, even while she suffered as well.

"Tell me," Guy said at last, "that this *is* a joke."

Jana gave him a wan smile and shook her head. "I wish I could," she said earnestly.

"How long?" His words came out frozen like ice.

"About five months, she says." She shrugged. "Dorothy asked me to come and let you know."

"Naturally," Guy said bitterly, "Edie felt I was the last person on earth who should be informed."

Jana said nothing because there was nothing to say. She stared unblinkingly at her hands.

"Does Miles know?" he asked in a raspy voice.

"I really couldn't say," she answered quietly, "but I don't think he does."

"He'll have to marry her!"

Jana shook her head and wearily rubbed her hand across her forehead. She had a splitting headache, and now that she had told Guy, she wanted nothing more than to end this dreadful meeting and go away where she could be alone.

"No, he can't," she said dully. "He can't marry her . . . not for a long while, anyway. I . . . I believe I'm pregnant, too, Guy."

There was a heavy silence for a long minute. Then, without a word, Guy came to her, gently pulled her out of the chair and into his arms. "You poor kid," he said softly. "You poor kid. This mess is even worse for you than for me. What are you going to do, Jana?"

She shrugged as he released her. "I don't know yet. I honestly just don't know."

At home again, Jana went upstairs and began removing her clothes once more from the dressing room off Miles's bedroom. She had done that, what . . . once, twice since she had been back? It didn't matter. This was the final time. After today there was no question of her ever allowing Miles to make love to her again, no question of their ever sharing a bedroom again.

Love. What a strange word people used to cover such a wide range of emotions and actions. In the name of love, they could do such cruel things to one another, could cause so much pain and suffering.

She finished arranging her clothes in the closet in the spare room. Then she went back downstairs to make herself a cup of strong, hot tea, which she carried into the living room.

She was still sitting there an hour later when Miles arrived. The room was shrouded in the gathering gloom of evening because Jana had not thought to turn on a light.

"Hey, what are you doing in the dark?" Miles asked cheerfully when he saw her after he had flipped on a lamp near the door. "Did you fall asleep? Really, precious heart, you're turning into such a sleepyhead these days I'm beginning to worry about you. Maybe you ought to see a doctor."

"I wasn't asleep," she answered in a dull voice. "I was just thinking."

"Serious thinking by the look of you." He crossed the room to the table with the liquor decanters. "You didn't make the drinks," he observed. "Do you want one?" He pulled out the stopper in one of the bottles and splashed a liberal portion of Scotch into a glass.

"No." Jana's cup of tea had long since been forgotten on the table beside her. But though she had been deeply engrossed in her thoughts, she still had not arrived at any kind of a decision.

Miles carried his drink as he went to drop down on the sofa near her. He set it on the lamp table while he tugged at his tie until it hung loosely around his neck and the top button of his shirt was opened. Then he sighed, picked up his glass, and leaned back against the cushions as he relaxed and took a sip of the drink.

From beneath partially lowered eyelashes Jana watched him. Almost dispassionately she observed the most minute details about his appearance—the strong, yet finely molded, outline of his head, the slight disarray of his dark hair, the length of his dark eyelashes that were now concealing his eyes. Even his hands. They were large hands that looked capable of handling almost anything. As he raised his glass to his lips again, she caught a glimpse of the narrow gold band encircling the ring finger on his left hand. His wedding ring. A ring of promise . . . an unkept promise.

And yet she was not as unaffected by his presence as she thought, because when he lifted his head and smiled warmly at her, in spite of everything her traitorous heart skipped a beat. It had always been that way, she thought, brooding. All Miles Parrish had ever had to do was just smile at her in that special, intimate way and all her defenses crumbled just as the walls of Fort Sumter had beneath the red-hot mortar fire of Confederate guns so long ago.

But, like the soldiers who had so bravely defended that fortress, Jana refused to surrender. The Union forces had, finally, but she never would! Her heart must be protected against the assault of Miles's magnetism at all costs. Resolutely, she looked away from him without returning his smile.

"How was your day?" he asked pleasantly.

Jana shrugged.

Miles tried again. "What's for dinner?"

Suppressed emotions suddenly welled and bubbled within her, and Jana laughed, shrilly, unsteadily. "Peach pie," she replied, giggling.

"That's it?"

"That's it." Jana nodded and briefly met his penetrating gaze. "If it's not enough, you'll just have to fix something else yourself." She laughed again at the thought of the pie and what a happy idiot she had been when she had baked it.

Unexpectedly, Miles was suddenly looming over her, his dark face menacing as it was thrust close to hers while his hands on the chair's arms braced his body above her. "Jana." His voice was knife-sharp, commanding. "What's wrong with you tonight? Have you been drinking?"

"No. I'm quite, quite sober. More's the pity." The giggling that had for a moment verged on the hysterical ceased as abruptly as it had begun. "Get away from me, Miles," she said coolly. "I don't want you near me."

Miles recoiled at once, and shock swept across his face like a storm moving in from the ocean. "What *is* wrong with you?" he demanded again as he stood upright before her. "You're behaving so strangely."

"If I am," she said icily, "perhaps it's only because at last I realize the true extent of my stupidity. And it's been colossal! I've moved out of our bedroom again, Miles. This time for good."

Something flared deep within his black eyes, but it was gone too quickly for her to decide whether it had been alarm or anger. Miles sucked in a sharp breath, brushed a hand over his face, and sat down again. But his eyes did not leave her face for even a fraction of an instant.

"What is it now?" he asked in a voice that was as cold as hers had been. "Last night everything was fine. We were happy and we went to sleep wrapped in each other's arms. Now you're telling me again that it's over between us. I'm getting just a little tired of our on-again, off-again style of marriage, Jana. You really are going to have to make up your mind."

"You weren't listening," she said shortly. "I have made up my mind. I never want you to touch me again. Not even so much as a handshake."

Miles laughed, but he was not amused. "Since when did we ever shake hands?" he taunted. "All we ever did was make love—when we weren't fighting, anyway."

"I don't even want to fight with you anymore,"

Jana said, suddenly listless again. "I only want you to leave me alone."

"What sin am I supposed to have committed this time?" Miles's voice was sarcastic, and there was an ugly sneer twisting his lips.

Jana stared at him. He was angry with *her* when it was his own actions that had brought them to this point. He was sitting there glaring at her in outrage, even righteous indignation, just as though he were a wronged man, a man pushed to the outer limits of his endurance. She shook her head in disbelief. It was incredible—*Miles* was incredible—and now she thought for the first time, in astonishment, that she had never known him at all!

She wondered whether he knew yet about Edie's news. Guy had asked her that this afternoon, and she had told him she didn't think so. She still didn't. Surely Miles could not be here attempting to come across so innocently if he did know. Surely even he could not be such a great actor as to carry *that* off with the aggrieved air of a much-put-upon man!

But she had no intention of enlightening him herself. She had already done enough this day by telling Guy, by absorbing the impact of it all upon her own life. She felt no sense of duty when it came to informing Miles as well. Let him find out from someone else . . . Edie, for instance. She had not had the courage to face Guy with her news, but at least she should be the one to tell Miles. It was going too far to expect her, Jana, to do that, too!

Again she shook her head. "I'm in no mood to discuss the matter with you, Miles," she answered at last. She got to her feet, feeling more weary, more drained, than she ever remembered being in her life. "I'm tired and I'm going to bed."

Miles was on his feet in a flash, and he grabbed her arms. "You can't do this," he growled. "I at least deserve the courtesy of some sort of explanation from you!"

"You deserve nothing!" Jana flared back in her first show of spirit all evening. "Get your hands off me. I told you not to touch me again, not ever, and I meant it!"

"And I don't take orders from you!" Miles snapped. "You're my wife, and I'll touch you whenever I please! You are *not* going to hold me at arm's length ever again, Jana, and that's a promise!"

Ruthlessly, he pulled her into his arms, and his lips parted just before seizing hers. His mouth was hard and bruising upon hers, with no vestige whatever of tenderness. This was no kiss of sweetly shared passion but rather a brutal, punishing assault upon her soft lips, an attack upon her already battered emotions.

Appalled, Jana tried to free herself, but the more she struggled, the more painful his embrace became. Now, with utter disregard for her feelings, his hands raked up and down her body, traveling from her breasts to her hips and then over her back, only to begin again. All the time the endless plundering of her mouth continued, until finally Jana could no longer fight. She went limp in his arms; her mouth was passive beneath his and her head spun dizzily.

At last he lifted his head, and his eyes smoldered as they met her pain-clouded gray ones. But it was Jana who spoke first.

"So now," she said lifelessly, "you would add rape to our relationship."

So quickly that she stumbled backward, Miles released her. "Never!" he answered raggedly. His breathing was heavy, labored. "I was trying to show you . . ."

"That physically you can overpower me?" Her voice was thick with scorn. "If that's the way you want me, then take me, Miles. But if you do, I will hate you until my dying day."

"You're mistaken," he said with such a chilling anger that it caused her to shiver. "I don't want you at all anymore."

He turned and grabbed his suit jacket from where he had tossed it across the arm of the sofa. Then long strides carried him to the door.

Chapter Eight

She awoke in heavy darkness with a keen awareness of the sharp hunger pains that assailed her. Jana attempted to ignore them and closed her eyes in the hope that blissful sleep would claim her in its warm arms again. But her stomach rumbled noisily and insistently, and she even felt a little nauseated. And then she remembered that she had not eaten at all the previous day except for a late breakfast. She remembered, too, her suspicions of pregnancy; if they had any basis, she had no business going without food. It might harm the baby.

She flipped on the bedside lamp, glanced at the clock, and saw that it was well past two. What an hour for a meal! She grinned to herself as she threw back the covers, patted her midsection gently, and got to her feet. She *was* pregnant, of course. She was as certain about that as she was of her own existence, and this child was already a stickler about having regular meals, clock or no clock.

After she slipped on a robe, she went downstairs to the kitchen and began rummaging through the refrigerator. There was little there, since she had not prepared a meal last night, and the sight of the pie sickened her. What, she wondered with only the mildest curiosity, had Miles eaten for his dinner?

She found some leftover roast Daisy had cooked the day before yesterday, and she made a sandwich with some of it and poured a glass of milk.

The gurgling sounds of starvation abated as she ate, and when she had finished, she felt much better. It was amazing what only a little food could do. Her mind felt sharper, clearer, and even though her problems remained, her spirits felt lighter somehow.

She had no idea whether or not Miles had returned during the night. Right after he had left, she had gone to bed and had fallen at once into an exhausted and dreamless sleep. The emotional storm of the day had completely drained her. But now she felt wide awake and alert, and the wheels of her mind were turning once more.

Last night had been dreadful. When Miles had kissed her—no, when he had *assaulted* her with his attentions—she had hated him violently. Even worse, she had hated herself because, though she had fought him, had tried to resist him, though she had known it was not a tender act of love on his part, she had responded inside herself! His mere touch could reduce her to such spinelessness, and she detested herself for being so vulnerable. It was shameful, and it proved that where Miles was concerned she had a contemptible lack of pride.

He had had no idea, of course, of the fire of desire that had raged through her, rendering her weak and helpless. She was grateful for that, at least. True, after her carefully calculated words to him later he had left her in cold anger. But that did not matter.

This way he would keep his distance from her, and for now that was enough.

She thought with sudden longing of Holly and of her snug little apartment. She had raced there once before to hide from Miles, and she yearned to do it again, now, tonight. But the problem was more complicated than it had been the first time. Now there was her baby to be considered before she made any move. She must not act rashly or do anything without first considering the consequences to her child. Although she was still healthy and strong at the moment and was quite capable of going to work to support herself, in the months ahead the situation would change. She would grow large and awkward, and once the baby was actually born, she would not be able to work for a while.

There was a sudden rattling noise at the kitchen door, and Jana jerked around to stare at it in fear. Someone was trying to break into the house! A silent scream rose in her throat, but she made no sound as she jumped to her feet, ran for the telephone, and lifted the receiver. But before she could dial the operator, the door opened and Miles walked into the room.

Fear drained away slowly and in its place came a mixture of anger and relief. "Miles Parrish!" she exclaimed as she grabbed the edge of the counter to keep herself from falling with her jelly-limp legs. "You terrified me! I thought you were a burglar!"

"I'm sorry. I thought you'd have gone to bed long ago." Dark circles of fatigue beneath his eyes gave Miles the appearance of an ill man, along with his colorless face, mussed hair, and rumpled clothes.

They stared at each other in silence for what seemed like forever, both sober, wary, assessing the other. Again, against her will, Jana felt the tug of his magnetism. Her senses throbbed at his nearness, and an ache of regret and loss hammered at her heart. She loved him, no matter what he had done, and she supposed, sadly, that she always would.

Miles broke the silent spell. "What are you doing up at this hour, anyway?"

"I was hungry, so I came down for a sandwich." She half expected him to make some teasing comment about how she was always hungry these days, but he didn't, and she asked, "Did you ever eat anything yourself?"

Miles shook his head. "I didn't think of it," he admitted. He looked so haggard and broken that, in spite of her resistance, Jana was disarmed.

"I'll make you a sandwich," she said quietly. She turned toward the refrigerator.

"No," Miles said from behind her. "I'm really not hungry. Jana, I've got to say something to you. I've been out walking for hours, thinking about us, and I know you suddenly hate me again for some reason, but I've got to say this anyway."

He paused and Jana froze, listening, still facing away from him. "I love you," Miles said after a long time. His voice was heavy and strained. "Tell me what I've done, what I can do to change things. I love you and I don't want to lose you . . . ever."

Tears filled Jana's eyes, and she caught her lower lip between her teeth to hold it steady. Pain sped through her veins like a poison, and, slowly, she shook her head.

"It's too late," she said hoarsely. "Far too late." And it was. Dear God, she thought, how desperately she had wanted him to say those words to her of late. But now he was saying them and they were meaningless. Even if Miles believed what he was saying, it was no good. There was still Edie and his responsibility to her, as well as his responsibility to his wife.

It was too late for love to be a consideration for any of them.

One week later, Jana walked out of the medical clinic into the bright warm sunlight. Her pregnancy had been confirmed.

Her emotions were turbulent as she walked to her car. Outwardly, she knew, she had never looked better than she did today in her soft aqua-blue spring dress, and with her silky hair swaying gently against her neck. The few pounds she had gained filled out her face and figure becomingly. Her bones were not quite so prominent, and there was a healthy glow in her cheeks that had not been placed there by cosmetics. She looked good. Physically, she felt excellent, and the doctor had teased her about being hearty pioneer stock since she had not yet suffered the slightest disposition to morning sickness. He had patted her on the shoulder, congratulated her, and prophesied that her entire pregnancy would be trouble-free.

Trouble-free. If only life itself were trouble-free! How she wished that, like any other young married woman, she could be thrilled and excited about her impending motherhood, confident that her husband would be equally joyous.

Jana got into her car and a moment later pulled out into the street, heading in the direction of the restaurant where she had promised to meet Caroline for lunch. Caroline had called last night to say she was visiting her mother and had asked if Jana was free today. Ordinarily, Jana would have enjoyed nothing more than seeing her friend, but today she was less than enthusiastic. No matter how much she loved Caroline, when all was said and done she was still Miles's sister. Today Jana would have to care-

fully guard her tongue so that she would not accidentally reveal her news. Before anyone else in the
family could be told, she had to speak to Miles first.

A frown marred her brow as she paused at a traffic
light. The way things were these days, she might
need to make an appointment at his office in order to
see him. Ever since that night when he had come
back so late and had told her he loved her and she
had been forced to reject him, she had scarcely even
seen him. He left early in the morning and came
home late in the evening. During the short periods
when he was around, only an icy silence existed
between them. Entirely gone as though they had
never occurred were the days of warm closeness
between them.

Oddly enough, Miles had not mentioned a separation. Jana could only suppose he assumed she would
give him the same argument she had before: that she
would stay until next year's election because of her
promise to Dorothy. The truth was she was staying
now only because she was frightened. She did not
know where to go or what to do now that she was
expecting a child. She did not want to go away
somewhere and be entirely alone, and it was out of
the question to stay with Holly again under the
present circumstances. In that moment, Jana
yearned for her own mother with such a deep
intensity that it shook her.

If Edie had yet told Miles about her news, Jana
had seen no visible signs of it. Miles did not in the
least wear the look of guilt about him. On the
contrary, he still acted as though he were the injured
party in their marriage—injured by her inexplicable
aloofness. As far as she was aware, Jana did not
think he had even been informed by his mother that
Edie was now living in her house. If he had called or

visited her this past week, either Dorothy had not told him or Miles had concealed his knowledge from his wife.

Jana sighed and turned a corner. She had spoken briefly to Dorothy only a few days ago herself, but the older woman had said little about Edie and Jana had not pursued the matter.

She arrived at the restaurant and was glad to be able to shove away her disturbing thoughts for a little while. She parked the car and walked quickly toward the entrance.

Caroline was waiting for her in the lobby, looking spectacularly beautiful in a white knit dress. Her black hair was draped over her shoulders, framing a face that was animated by an unmistakably delighted smile.

"Jana!" she exclaimed, rushing forward to embrace her. "I've been waiting ages! I thought you'd never come!"

"Sorry," Jana said contritely. "I was running late doing a few errands." Quickly, she changed the subject. Caroline was quite capable of asking what errands, and Jana was in no mood to invent any. "You're looking fabulous as usual, Caroline. Marriage is certainly agreeing with you."

Caroline laughed softly. "That it is." She backed away a step to observe Jana better and said, "You're looking pretty good yourself. I believe you've put on a little weight."

Jana felt her face beginning to redden and prayed that Caroline would not jump to logical conclusions "A pound or two," she admitted lightly. "I've been developing my cooking skills now that I'm no longer a working woman. Shall we go in?"

Caroline nodded and together they entered the restaurant, where a hostess led them to a table.

For a little while both women were occupied studying menus and ordering, but at last they were alone and free to talk.

"How is it Bill allowed you to leave him alone for a few days?" Jana asked in a teasing vein. "I would have thought you'd still be too busy honeymooning for a separation yet."

Caroline grinned at her. "It was a forced separation. He had to make a trip to New York to see some other lawyers about some case. So I decided to come home for a few days rather than stay there all alone in the apartment."

"I'm glad you did. I'm sure Dorothy is, too. We all miss you."

Caroline nodded. "I wish it were possible for us to live here, but of course it isn't. I'm beginning to make friends in Columbia, so it's not been too lonely for me, but it isn't home. Oh," she added with excitement, "we've been house hunting, Jana! There's this one in particular that we both like, and if we can swing the loan, I think we're going to buy it!"

Until their food arrived, Caroline favored Jana with a minute description of the house and how she planned to furnish it. When she had finished, Jana had a feeling that if she walked into the house blindfolded, she would probably be able to locate every closet and find every electrical outlet. But, tedious as it was, since she was hardly as enthusiastic about the house's charms as Caroline was, Jana was happy to let her talk about it. It kept them from discussing more personal matters.

But that state of affairs could not last forever. Inevitably Caroline finally ran out of steam about her dream home. They had finished their salads, and as she sliced into her steak Caroline sighed. "This is so nice, Jana, our being able to meet for lunch. But I sort of feel guilty about enjoying myself so much while Mom is stuck at home with only Edie for company."

Jana picked up a packet of sugar to pour into her tea and gazed absently at it. She remembered the doctor's caution about empty carbohydrates and put it down again. "You should have invited her to come along," she replied.

Caroline made a wry face. "I thought of it. But if I had, she would have felt duty-bound to bring Edie, too. And that would have spoiled our lunch."

Silently Jana agreed, but aloud she only said, "Well, it was Dorothy's idea to have her move in."

"I know." Caroline shrugged. "And I can understand why she did it. She *is* Guy's wife, after all. But honestly, Jana, she's pure misery to be around. All she does is sit around crying or whining and feeling sorry for herself. She really is ill about half of each day with her morning sickness, and she looks awful. But even so, she's just not trying! She won't bother with make up. Mom says some days she doesn't even get dressed. And she's always going on about how everyone has always misunderstood her, never tried to understand her side of anything, and about how mean Guy is being to her now. My gosh, she goes on and on just as though she never did a thing to hurt this family! Sometimes I could just shake her! How Mom is going to stand it for months on end I just can't imagine."

Neither could Jana, if Edie were still carrying on the way she had on the last two occasions she had seen her. Such a flood of tears! It was almost as though Edie actually enjoyed her unhappiness, silly as that sounded.

"I suppose," Jana ventured, "that your mother

told you she sent me to tell Guy about Edie's condition. When I spoke with her a few days ago, she said he still had not called or come. Has he yet?''

"No," Caroline said in exasperation, "and to tell you the truth, Jana, I could wring his neck! Stubborn as a mule, he is! When I called him about Edie's support money a couple of weeks ago after Miles asked me to, he was hateful and rude and told me to keep my nose out of his business. But even so, I never thought he'd be so cruel as to stay away once he learned he was going to be a father! I mean, a person can carry a grudge just so far. You'd think he'd be a little interested in his own child, wouldn't you?"

Guy's child? *Guy's child!* Jana was so astounded she almost exclaimed it aloud. But then she became aware that her friend was looking at her in an odd way. Flustered, Jana picked up her unsweetened tea and took a sip.

The waitress stopped at the table at that moment to ask if everything was all right. Caroline answered her, and that gave Jana a breathing space, an instant to pull herself together. She supposed it was entirely within the realm of possibility that Edie was, in fact, having Guy's child. After all, they had still been living together as man and wife five months ago. But if that was the case, why should Edie be afraid to tell him herself? And why, too, would Guy have been so quick to jump to the wrong conclusion?

The flare of hope that had blazed inside her sputtered and died. No, Jana cautioned herself. It was self-defeating to pin hopes on nothing more substantial than Caroline's natural assumptions. And it was easy for Caroline to assume what she did. She had never for a minute believed Edie's story about an affair with Miles. But then, unlike Jana, she had never seen Edie in Miles's arms in the bedroom.

The possibility possessed Jana's mind for the rest of the afternoon. It was still there when she drove out to the factory at five. During one of their rare conversations during the past week, Miles had asked her to pick him up that day since his own car would be in the garage for a tune-up.

She slid her car into Miles's reserved parking space near the office building, cut the motor, and waited. But by five-twenty she grew impatient. If Miles didn't hurry, they would really be rushed later on. Tonight they were expected at a dinner honoring a state senator. If they didn't get home soon, they would have little time to dress for it.

She had just decided to give him five more minutes before going in to search for him when Miles emerged from the building and strode quickly toward the car. Jana slid from beneath the steering wheel over to the passenger side of the seat.

"I hope I didn't make you wait too long," Miles said apologetically as he took her former position beneath the steering wheel. "There were a few last-minute problems."

"It's okay," she answered stiffly, glancing straight ahead through the window. "But I was beginning to worry about our getting home in time to dress for the dinner tonight. I thought maybe you had forgotten about it."

"No, I didn't forget."

There was a little silence between them, awkward, yet full-bodied. Jana hated it. She hated the way things were now, and yet there was nothing she could do to change them. Even so, as Miles drove through the gate and guided the car into the mainstream of traffic, she asked tentatively, "Have all the rumors finally died and been buried?"

"More or less." He gave his head a weary shake. "At least, I've not heard any more about it. I just

wish I could find out where those stories originated
. . . and why."

"Do you think it's politically motivated?" she
asked.

"It could easily be," Miles agreed. "All sorts of
stories get going when people run for office, but it
seems utterly ridiculous at this point. It's still so
early that I'm not even a declared candidate yet, and
neither is anyone else. Besides that, it's not exactly a
scandalous story . . . just one to stir up the employees and worry them about their security."

"It doesn't make any sense," Jana acknowledged.

"Well"—Miles's tone of voice changed—"I'm
tired of that subject anyway. All I want is to forget it
and hope it never rears its ugly little head again.
What," he asked conversationally, "did you do
today?"

"Lunched with Caroline."

Miles shot her a look of mild surprise. "What's she
doing in town?"

"Spending a few days with Dorothy while Bill is
away on a business trip."

Miles kept his eyes on the traffic, but Jana noticed
his jaw harden as he asked, "Is she still floating on
her honeymoon cloud?"

"Yes. They're trying to buy a house." She sighed.
"She spent half an hour telling me every little detail
about the place."

For the first time in days, Miles chuckled in her
presence. "Talked your ear off, did she?" He shook
his head. "I love my sister, but, to tell the truth, I
don't know how you can endure her for very long at
a time. Her enthusiasms wear me out."

Jana laughed. "Sometimes they wear me out, too,
but I guess I can't blame her for being so excited
about her first home. I remember how thrilled I was
when we bought our house."

Another awkward silence developed, and Jana could have bitten off her tongue. Why had she said that? she wondered, furious at herself. There was no good purpose in bringing up such memories to torture them both.

They did not speak again. When they reached the house, she rushed inside ahead of Miles, eager to get away from him and the disturbing visions that she had unfortunately brought into focus. She remembered the two of them on the day the house had legally become theirs, walking through each room with their arms around each other. Softly, they had discussed their plans for the house, their hopes and dreams concerning their marriage, and the children they would have. With the exception of their wedding day, to Jana it had been the most beautiful and memorable day they had ever shared. But now the thought of it brought unbearable pain, and she had been afraid that if she had stayed in Miles's presence even a single minute more, she would have broken down.

In the privacy of her bedroom, Jana got her emotions under control. Sitting on the edge of the bed, she sucked in deep, sharp breaths until finally some of the tension left. The tears that scorched her throat receded, and her trembling hands stilled. Once she was sufficiently calm, she went to take her shower, and the hot water helped to wash away even more of her tenseness. By the time she returned to her room to dress, she felt almost normal again.

Discarding her robe, she pulled on a pair of silky panty hose and then hooked her strapless bra into place. A black half-slip was smoothed down over hips and thighs. Jana glanced toward the dresser mirror and turned sideways.

Her middle was only the tiniest bit swelled; no one else could possibly detect her secret by just looking at her. But she could see the difference herself. And all at once a great surge of tenderness engulfed her. She was having a child—Miles's child—and no matter what else happened, she could never be sorry for that. She loved him and she loved the child she was carrying, and no one could ever deny her the exquisite joy his baby would bring to her.

She felt fiercely protective of her baby and, remembering her own unhappy childhood, she swore to herself that she would not allow her child to ever be hurt by anyone. When she and Miles divorced, she would raise her child alone. Certainly no cruel stepfather would ever have an opportunity to lay a finger on it. No child would ever receive more love and understanding than hers, for she would give her all.

For the evening ahead she had decided upon a black silk dress. She had chosen it because it was loose-fitting in the waist and hips. It would be comfortable as well as flattering with its long, full sleeves that bloused above the wrists and gathered beneath tiny white cuffs. But there was one problem. The dress had small, fabric-covered buttons that fastened up the back, and Jana could not do them herself. She had only worn it once or twice before in Atlanta, and Holly had obligingly helped her then. Now Jana fumbled, her back half turned toward the mirror as she peered over her shoulder, attempting to see what she was doing.

In frustration, she was just about to give up and search the closet for another dress when the door opened.

Miles, immaculate in a dark suit, filled the doorway, and Jana caught her breath as their eyes met.

"I came to see if you're ready," he said, "but you appear to be having trouble."

"I . . . I'll be ready in a few more minutes," she promised. Ineffectively, her fingers continued to work at her back.

Miles came toward her. "Turn around," he ordered quietly.

"No, thanks. I can manage."

"I said turn around." Something hot flashed in his eyes, as though he were gearing up for battle.

Wisely, Jana submitted. Without another word, she turned her back to him and then struggled to ignore the sensations that raced through her as his fingers touched the bare skin of her back.

Suddenly the fingers stilled. Without warning, Miles's lips scorched her back as they made a small trail up her spine.

"Jana," he whispered huskily.

"No!" She went rigid. "No!" She jerked from him, away from the touch that ravaged her senses and demolished her resolve. She could not allow herself ever to be weak again.

"I've had all I'm going to take!" Miles grated in quick fury. His eyes glittered like two hot coals. "I don't care about your promise to Mom. I don't care about any election. I don't *care* about anything anymore!" He was practically shouting. "I will *not* go on living like a monk, with my wife right here in the same house! If you won't be a wife to me, Jana, then I'm calling it quits! Only, this time you don't have to move out. I will, first thing tomorrow." His jaw became like cement. Then he added in a lower voice as he obviously struggled to control his aroused emotions, "Now I think we'd better go. We're late as it is."

Jana did not know how she did it. But at the gathering they attended, she smiled, shook hands, smiled some more, and even made small talk. All the while she was bleeding inside. *Miles was leaving her!* The thought tumbled over and over in her head like a piece of cork tossed by ocean waves. He would leave, and there was nothing she could do to stop him.

And yet wasn't that what she wanted? Certainly she had no intention of staying with him after the baby was born. But then, Miles did not know about that. She couldn't tell him until she had reached a firm decision about her plans for herself and her baby's future.

Most of the evening Jana saw little of Miles. Both of them circulated among the other guests, and she did her best to be sociable. But by ten o'clock she felt sick with exhaustion from the effort of pretending to enjoy herself. A headache pounded against her temples, and she looked around, searching for Miles. If he weren't ready to leave yet himself, she would take a cab home. She knew she could not endure the smoke-filled room and the din of numerous conversations a moment longer.

At first she could not see Miles anywhere. Then she saw him enter the living room from the library, where some of the men had gone for a private talk. One glimpse of his darkened face told her something besides their own soured marriage was wrong.

Miles's own gaze raked the room. When he spotted her, he deftly wove his way through the throng of milling guests and reached her side.

"Are you ready to leave?" he asked abruptly.

"Very," she replied. "I was just looking for you for the same reason." Unable to stop herself, she touched his arm, lowered her voice, and asked, "Miles, what's wrong?"

He shook his head. "Not now. Let's find our hosts and say our good-byes."

Ten minutes later, Miles's hand on her elbow, they left the house. It was a warm night, but a small breeze blowing in from the harbor caressed Jana's face and fluttered her hair. They reached the car, and Miles opened her door for her.

Only when they were both inside did Miles speak. "Do you," he began, and his voice shook with anger, "remember us talking just this afternoon about who might have started those rumors about the company?"

Bemused, Jana nodded.

Miles gave a ragged laugh. "You're not going to believe this, but it was my own dear brother!"

"Guy?" Jana gasped.

Miles practically snorted. "Do I have another?" He nodded in the shadowy darkness. "I just found out. David Sipes was asking me if it was true, and I said no. Then I happened to ask him where he had heard it, and he told me Guy was the one to tell him a couple of months ago."

"I just don't believe it," Jana said slowly, trying to digest the information.

"Well, I do." Miles started the ignition, grating, "And I intend to get to the bottom of this thing once and for all tonight."

The car shot down the street, tires squealing, and Jana shouted in alarm, "Slow down, for God's sake! What are you trying to do, get us killed?"

As the car careened around a corner Miles ignored her, only slowing down to a safer speed at last when he was forced to by other traffic. But his hands continued to grip the steering wheel in a way that suggested he wished he were throttling Guy's neck.

Jana quaked with fear. Already this evening Miles had been infuriated once. With this fresh anger at Guy, she was honestly worried that Miles *had* indeed been pushed beyond the limit—by herself and now by his brother.

Her mouth was dry and her voice cracked when she spoke. "Let's go home, Miles. Cool down and sleep on it; then see Guy tomorrow."

He shook his head and said implacably, "No, we're going to settle this score tonight. He's abused me all he's going to, and I've been a fool to let him get by with it. But it stops now!" The car sped up again, crossed into the opposite lane, and passed the car ahead of them.

When they reached Guy's apartment building, she hurried up the sidewalk beside Miles, thinking, *Maybe if I'm here it'll stop the two of them from murdering each other.* But she was not at all confident of her ability to stop impending disaster as Miles violently jabbed at the doorbell.

It was a sleepy, irritable Guy who opened the door. "What the . . . ?" he began when he saw the two of them. Then he blinked in disbelief and his mouth fell open as Miles pressed against the door and bulldozed his way inside.

Guy's gaze went swiftly to Jana, and there was a question mark in his eyes. She shrugged helplessly, and they both followed Miles into the living room.

Guy flicked on an overhead light. He had thrown a robe on over his bare chest and pajama bottoms, and now he sought to arrange it so that it covered him better. But as his hands tied the belt his eyes were unwaveringly on Miles, and he maintained a cautious distance.

"I suppose," he said unpleasantly, "that you've got a good reason for bursting in here like this."

"You bet I do," Miles said grimly. "I've come to give you a thrashing you'll never forget!"

Dark, angry color surged into Guy's face and, fully awake now, he doubled his hands into fists.

"Have you, now?" he said with a dangerous glint in his eyes. "We'll just see about that."

Miles took a menacing step toward Guy and growled, "I just learned tonight that you're the one who was responsible for all those rumors about a takeover of my company, about my being in bad financial straits. You've caused me no end of trouble, *little brother!*"

Guy scowled and lifted his fists. "That's right, *big brother!* I did start those stories, and I'd have done a lot more than that, even sabotaged the place, if I had known what I know now!"

"What the heck are you talking about?" Miles asked impatiently. "Are you still hung up on that ridiculous story Edie made up?"

"It's not a ridiculous story!" Guy snapped. "She's pregnant!"

"So? What do you expect me to do . . . congratulate you?" Miles was so patently unaffected by the pronouncement that both Guy and Jana were taken aback, and they gave each other a blank look. And then Miles, apparently catching the significance of their glances, exploded. "You can't think that! You don't!" The words were so loud that they reverberated from the walls and ceiling. "My God, Guy, are you completely mad? I've tried and tried to tell you I never touched your wife, but you wouldn't *listen* to me!" Now the wild fury of his gaze swept to Jana, and there was contempt in his eyes. "So that's the explanation of your latest touch-me-not edict! And I thought you, at least, had believed me when I told you Edie was lying, but you didn't, did you?" He bent forward in a mock bow. "Thank you," he said in a voice laced with sarcasm. "Thank you both for your great faith in me. And now, Guy, go get dressed." It was an arrogant command, not a request.

"Why?" Guy, uncertain now, yet still unconvinced even after the volcanic tirade, glared sullenly at his brother.

"Because," said Miles, "we're all going to see Edie right now and get this whole thing straightened out. I don't know why she lied, but she's done enough of it to last a lifetime—and even if I have to spank her, I'll have the truth out of her tonight!"

Chapter Nine

There was only a brief conversation in the car when Miles started off in the direction of the highway. Jana quickly told him that Edie was not at the island house but at Dorothy's. Miles lifted his eyebrows in vague surprise and without a word altered his course, and they drove silently through the dark streets.

It was nearing midnight, and Jana was sure they would rouse the household from sleep. But when they parked in front of the house, lights filtered from the front windows.

At this time of night the doors were locked, and Miles pressed impatiently on the bell. Behind him stood a silent, angry Guy and a nervous Jana. What, she wondered with dread, would be the final outcome of all this? For some reason, she had a premonition that it would not be a happy one.

Caroline answered the door and blinked in astonishment. "Did someone forget to tell me we're having a midnight Parrish clan meeting?" she quipped.

No one responded to her little joke. Miles and Guy strode wordlessly past her, and she gave Jana a look of wide-eyed curiosity. "What's going on?" she demanded.

"Your guess is as good as mine," Jana replied briefly. "They've come to see Edie."

"Well, for heaven's sake, let's get in there!" Caroline exclaimed. "We don't want to miss anything!"

Caroline hurried to follow her brothers into the living room, but Jana went more slowly. There had already been too many emotional episodes this night, and she was not looking forward to another. As keyed up and angry as both men were, there was no telling what would happen.

In the living room the scene was tense, expectant, and hushed. Dorothy, in a chair near the fireplace with an opened book on her lap, leaned forward. Caroline stood beside her, avid curiosity on her face as she watched the others. Edie, who sat on the sofa, was bundled in a floor-length pale blue robe, and her face was scrubbed clean of makeup, as though she had just emerged from her bath. It was the first time Jana had ever seen her without cosmetics. She was amazed at how much younger and more innocent-looking Edie appeared.

But she also looked terrified as the two brothers loomed in front of her. Guy was pasty-faced, while Miles was grimly intimidating.

"You've been silent about your lies long enough, Edie," Miles barked at her, "but tonight it ends. You're going to tell every member of this family the truth, or, by God, you'll live to regret it! Guy believes you're having *my* baby!"

Edie gasped with shock, and her eyes flew to her

husband's strained, white face. "Oh, no!" she cried brokenly. "Oh, no, Guy! That's not true! It's ours . . . yours!"

Guy stared at her, a man who had just had the breath knocked out of him. "Mine?" His voice cracked; then he threw a suspicious glance at Miles before looking down at his wife again. "But you said you and Miles were . . ."

"I know, I know!" Inevitable tears flooded Edie's eyes, and her gaze was fearful as she looked at Miles's stony face. She sucked in a deep breath and plunged. "I lied. I'm so sorry, Guy. Nothing ever happened between us. Like Miles said, I lied."

"I always said she had," Caroline murmured smugly from her position near her mother's chair.

"Hush!" Dorothy hissed.

The three involved in the dramatic tableau that was unfolding did not appear to have overheard the brief exchange. They were intent only upon themselves.

Slightly dazed, Guy shook his head. "But why?" he asked in a tortured voice. "It doesn't make sense, Edie. Did you hate me so much?"

"No!" Edie sobbed. "It was because . . . I loved you so much!"

"Now that's what I like," Caroline said irrepressibly. "Cool logic."

"Shut *up*, Caroline," Dorothy ordered from beneath her breath, "or I'll send you from the room!"

Caroline threw a wicked grin at Jana, but Jana did not share her amusement. She was just as stunned as the two men, and she stared at Edie, wishing she would stop crying long enough to explain.

Miles must have shared her frustrated impatience, because he said sternly, "Get a grip on yourself, Edie, and clear this thing up!"

Edie sniffed and wiped at her eyes. With a muffled

curse, Miles jerked out his handkerchief and threw it down onto her lap. Edie took it and began mopping her wet cheeks.

At last she looked at Guy, and though her voice was still unsteady, she was much more in control of her emotions. "You were always gone so much," she said plaintively. "Always working, always attending some meeting or other. I got so lonely."

"I was trying," he answered in a rigid voice, "to make a living for you. You wanted that house on the island, trips, things that cost a lot of money. I *had* to work all the time!"

Edie blanched at the harshness of his words. "Then . . . you should have told me," she stammered. "I didn't *have* to have that house or the other things. I didn't understand, Guy. I thought you *wanted* to stay away from home all the time."

"Wanted?" There was a world of agony in the one word.

The two of them stared at each other in surprise and dawning awareness for a long moment until finally Miles insisted, "Get on with it, Edie."

"Oh." Edie withdrew her gaze from Guy and looked down at the damp handkerchief balled in her hand. "I . . . well, I was scared and hurt. I thought you"—now she briefly met Guy's eyes again—"were seeing someone else. So . . . I decided to try to make you jealous and win you back again." She sighed heavily into the silence and doggedly forced herself to continue. "Since Miles and I had once been engaged, I thought you'd believe me if I said we were having an affair . . . so I did. But honestly, Guy, I never thought it would drive you away! I just hoped it would bring you back!"

"I'll bet medical science would be interested in the working processes of her brain," Caroline muttered.

This time either Dorothy did not hear or chose to

ignore her daughter's outburst, for her gaze never once flickered from Edie's face.

"And you mean to tell me that you and Miles didn't, haven't . . ." Words failed Guy.

Edie vigorously shook her head. "Never, I swear it! I've never loved any man except you, and no man has ever touched me but you. Please . . ." Her voice quivered and fresh tears glittered in her eyes. "Please, Guy, you have to believe me! I'm so . . . I'm so un . . . unhappy!"

"Sweetheart!" Guy melted and sank down beside her on the sofa and gathered her into his arms. "I believe you, darling," he said tenderly, "so stop crying. Everything is going to be all right now."

"She's not quite done yet," Miles said coldly.

Guy tossed him a withering look. "Leave her alone, Miles. Can't you see how upset she is?"

"That's just too bad," Miles said unfeelingly. "She's upset quite a few people herself. Edie, tell Jana why you were in our bedroom kissing me that day last year."

"In Miles's bedroom?" Guy drew back from his wife as though she were a deadly black widow spider. "Kissing?"

Edie looked at Jana with an apology in her eyes. "It wasn't what it looked like, truly," she began earnestly. "I knew Miles was home sick with the flu, and I wanted to talk to him about Guy. I thought maybe if he knew how much Guy was away from home, he would have a talk with him, help me somehow, because he and Guy were so close. I just walked into the house the way we always do in this family. Miles wasn't downstairs, so I went up and found him in the bedroom." She lowered her gaze to her hands again. "Miles was always good to me when we were engaged. He had always been willing to help me out of a jam, and I honestly didn't think anything about seeing him in the bedroom. I just wanted to talk to him. And when he promised to talk to Guy and said he was sure things would straighten out between us, I just kissed him without thinking . . . from gratitude . . . nothing more, I swear!" Now she lifted her eyes to Jana. "Only, you saw us and ran away. I felt terrible after I learned you'd left Miles for good. I felt I was to blame, but I couldn't tell you the truth, because nobody knew where you were." She sighed. "Later, when things worsened between Guy and me, I claimed Miles was my lover. I didn't think about it affecting you, because you weren't even here, and since Miles was living a bachelor life, I didn't believe it would hurt him, either. I never dreamed Guy would take it the way he did, that it would cause all this awful trouble. All I ever wanted was to get Guy's attention!"

"Attention?" Caroline burst out. "The entire Parrish family has been living its very own soap opera because of you!"

Edie promptly started sobbing again. Guy wrapped a protective arm around her shoulders while snapping, "That's enough out of you, Caroline! Come on, darling, let me get you upstairs where you can rest properly. All this crying can't be good for our baby."

"Oh, Guy. I'm sorry. I love you so much and I never meant . . ." Edie sniffled as he lifted her to her feet.

"Shhh," he murmured gently. "Forget it, darling. You've been a silly little goose, but no harm's done."

"No harm!" Caroline exclaimed in astonishment after the reunited lovebirds were gone. "She's had everyone believing outlandish lies, caused a separation between Miles and Jana, had Guy suing her for divorce and ready to murder his own brother. And now *he* tells *her* there's no harm done? If that doesn't take the cake!"

Dorothy rose to her feet. "Caroline, I told you before, I've had enough of your spicy comments for one night. Now come with me. I believe Miles and Jana would like to be alone."

Jana and Miles gazed at each other, both of them frozen and expressionless. Jana was only dimly aware of a protesting Caroline being forcibly evicted from the room by her frail-looking mother.

After they were gone, silence thundered through the room. Jana's heart hammered in her throat. She was searching Miles's face, memorizing every line of strain and suffering that had been etched across his forehead and around his eyes during the past year. His face was colorless and inflexible, like a cold, lifeless marble statue, and the only visible signs of life were his burning eyes that seared her soul.

She had been so wrong all along, right from the start. If only she had paused that day last year long enough to listen to an explanation, but she had not. She had believed the evidence of her eyes and that had been enough to send her rushing pell-mell away from Charleston, away from the man she loved. The man she still loved so desperately.

She had to tell him now. She had to beg his forgiveness, but the withdrawn expression in his eyes frightened her. It was not going to be easy.

Jana licked her lips and tried to swallow over the thick lump that clogged her throat. "Miles . . ." Her voice broke, and she paused, swallowed once more, and tried again. "Miles, what can I say? I'm sorry. So very sorry."

"Are you?" Miles's eyes glittered like black ice. "So am I, Jana. But your apology comes too late."

"Don't say that!" Fear dried her mouth. "Please,"

she pleaded, "I know how wrong I've been, but can't we start over?" The slight shake of his head further terrified her, and she rushed on in a tear-thickened voice. "I love you."

He shook his head vigorously this time, more decisively. "It's too late," he repeated in an emotionless voice that chilled her heart. "Love involves trust, and that's something you never could give me. We're through, Jana. I tried too long and too hard, but I don't even want to try anymore. All I wanted tonight was for you and Guy to finally know the truth, because I'm sick of carrying a load of blame for nothing. And now, if you'll excuse me, I'm leaving. I'll stay in a motel tonight. You can have the house if you want. This time there's no need for you to run away from Charleston unless you simply want to go." He inclined his head in a brief nod, just as though they were the barest of acquaintances. "Good-bye, Jana. It's been nice knowing you."

He was gone. Jana couldn't believe it, and yet it had happened. Miles had left her because he could not forgive her. Numbed, she was still standing in the same spot ten minutes later when Dorothy returned.

"Where's Miles?"

"He left me," Jana said, beyond prevarication.

Dorothy sighed. "I was afraid that would happen. Miles has a great deal of pride, and he's suffered greatly this past year. I had hoped by begging you to return to him until next year's elections to give you two plenty of time to work out your problems. But I was wrong to meddle. I love my son, and I love you like my own daughter, but I was wrong to try to influence your lives. You've both been hurt even more by my bringing you back, haven't you?"

Jana was too choked to reply, and finally Dorothy

took her by the arm. "Let's go upstairs," she suggested quietly. "You can sleep here tonight. You're in no shape to go home alone."

But Jana did not sleep. She lay thinking of Miles, of their shattered marriage, and of their baby. She still had not told him, and now she could not. Miles had a strong sense of duty, and if he knew about the baby, he might feel compelled to take her back for the child's sake. And no matter how much she loved him, Jana did not want Miles that way. It would then be a marriage of necessity, of expediency, and it would be a bleak life for them both. No, if it could not be a genuine marriage in every respect, it was better to end it now.

Only Guy knew about her pregnancy. The next day, after she had returned to her own empty house, Jana called him at his office and swore him to secrecy.

Guy, exuberantly happy over his reunion with Edie and his impending fatherhood, attempted to convince her that her own marriage could be the same. "Miles is just angry at us both for believing the worst about him. Give him a chance to simmer down, Jana, and I'm sure you can work things out. Look, I'll talk to him myself. I owe you that much."

"No." Jana's voice was flat. "You're not to tell him, Guy. I'll tell him myself, eventually, after the baby is born, but not now. I don't want him to feel pressured to stay married. It isn't fair to either of us. You have to promise me."

Guy's heavy sigh was a swooshing sound across the wire. "All right," he agreed reluctantly. "But where are you going?"

"Maybe back to Atlanta. But if Miles happens to ask, you don't know anything. You do owe me something, Guy, and it's to keep quiet."

One week later, Jana moved into a furnished apartment in Atlanta. During the previous days, despite Holly's invitation, she had stayed in a motel. Should any of the family try to reach her, she did not intend to be at Holly's, where she could be easily found. From her friend she had also extracted a firm promise not to betray her.

Only after she was settled in the apartment did she concentrate on the second necessity—finding a job. It was as though her mind, her emotions, were so dulled, so numbed, that she could only do one thing at a time.

She went to Allen Montgomery. There was no place else to go. She needed a job immediately so that she could work the remaining months until the baby's birth when she would be forced to take several weeks off. Not just anyone would be willing to hire her under such conditions, she realized.

Allen was astounded the day she walked into his office, and a flash of genuine delight lit his eyes. "Jana!" he exclaimed. "What a marvelous surprise. What in the world are you doing here?"

Jana attempted a smile, but she was not quite so calm as she wished to appear. "I've moved back to Atlanta," she told him, "and I came to apply for a job."

The smile left Allen's face. "What happened?" He peered intently at her, for the first time realizing that she was vastly different than she had been the last time he had seen her.

"It just didn't work out," she answered quietly, "and now we've separated for good. Allen, I really need a job. But before you decide whether or not to give me one, I have to be honest with you. I'm pregnant."

A swift frown creased the skin around his eyes. "Then what is Parrish doing by allowing you to go away from him?"

"He doesn't know."

"Doesn't *know?*" Allen barked. "Jana, you can't keep something like that from your own husband, for God's sake!"

"I can," she insisted, "and I will. Until after my child is born. Now, about that job . . ."

Allen raked a hand through his hair and stared at her. "You know you can have a job," he said almost impatiently, "but that's not the issue. You've got to tell him and . . ."

Jana shook her head. "Not yet. And the only way I'll work for you, badly as I need a job, is if you promise that if Miles contacts you, you won't tell him that I'm working for you or of my condition or where I am at all."

"That's not right."

"Promise," she said with a hint of steel in her voice, "or I'll go hunt for a job somewhere else."

"Damn it, you're *pregnant,* Jana! You shouldn't be working anywhere!"

But, in the end, her deep unhappiness and implacable will made him promise to keep her secret, just as she had elicited the same vow from both Holly and Guy.

The one bright spot during the next two months for Jana was her continued excellent health. Though Allen and Holly both fussed over her like two mother hens, Jana was careful to take good care of herself. She would do nothing to jeopardize her baby's health or her own. So she visited a doctor and took the vitamins he prescribed. She made sure she ate well-balanced meals three times a day whether she was hungry or not, and she watched her weight.

She paced herself at the office to keep from over-tiring, and most evenings she went to bed early.

Her new duties in Allen's company were in the marketing department. Since it was a new area for her, Jana appreciated the challenge. Just now learning something new was exactly what she needed. It kept her mind occupied with the business at hand and left little time for contemplating, at least during the day.

But the nights were different. Sometimes she spent an evening with Holly or went to dinner with Allen, and for a few hours her mind would be diverted from her personal problems. But most nights she was alone in her little apartment, and it was impossible not to think of Miles.

Although it was still unnecessary for her to wear maternity clothes, her middle now protruded notice-ably. One Saturday afternoon, Jana went out and shopped for a few loose-fitting blouses, slacks, and dresses that were smart enough for the office, yet still comfortable.

She was putting away her new purchases when the telephone rang. She knew it was either Allen or Holly, for they were the only people who knew her unlisted number.

It was Holly, and in her forthright manner she went straight to the point. "Miles just called—again. That makes four times since you came."

Jana went still and felt as though she were suffo-cating. "What . . . what did he say?"

"The same as before. He wants to find you. He sounded frantic."

"What did you tell him?" She gripped the receiver so tightly that her knuckles whitened.

"I've kept my promise, Jana," Holly answered wearily. "I told him I didn't know where you were. But I hate lying to him . . . and he knows I'm lying, or he wouldn't keep calling. He sounded so desperate to locate you. Why don't you call him?"

Jana shook her head, forgetting Holly couldn't see her. "I can't. I just can't talk to him yet."

"Are you so unforgiving?" Holly demanded. "Really, I never thought of you as the vindictive sort."

"I'm not!" Jana defended herself. "It isn't that, and you know it! But I'm just not ready to face Miles yet . . . or to talk to him. I've got all I can handle right now trying to survive, trying to sort out my life."

"Making mud of it is more like it," Holly muttered. She sighed. "All right, suit yourself, but I still say you're making a mistake. Anyway, I've passed on my message, so I'll go now."

Jana realized Holly was seriously upset with her, and she hated that. "Wait, Holly," she said quickly. "Why don't you come over tonight? I'll make dinner."

"Sorry. I've got a date."

"Some other time, then," Jana murmured.

After they hung up, she stared blankly at the pile of new clothes piled on the bed. Why did Miles keep trying to find her?

But almost as soon as the question entered her head, she had the answer. He had probably expected her to file for divorce, and when she had not, he wanted to do it himself. He was probably trying to locate her so that she could be served with the legal papers. Well, that was just too bad, she told herself furiously. He would just have to wait a few more months for his freedom.

She spent a miserable evening alone with her morose thoughts. Holly had been busy, but she had hoped that perhaps Allen would call or drop by as he often did. But the telephone remained obstinately silent, and no one came to the door. Jana busied herself with small tasks, hand-washing a few things, shampooing her hair, and doing her nails. All of it was an effort to keep her mind from dwelling on Miles.

When, she asked herself grimly as she prepared for bed, would she ever get him completely out of her system? When Holly had called today and mentioned his name, an aching longing had flooded through her. A picture of him tortured her mind. How she missed the vibrant, decisive, purposeful, energetic force of his presence! How she missed the odd little way he could lift an eyebrow whenever he was amused, and the way a slow, teasing smile would spread across his face, and the endearing way he used to call her "precious heart." Would such memories haunt her for the rest of her life?

Her sleep was restless that night, her dreams disturbing. She dreamed of Miles, a Miles who was furious with her, a Miles who was yelling at her, a Miles who hated her. And then he was pounding on something, and the dreadful noise jarred her awake.

But even with her eyes open in the predawn darkness, the pounding, thundering noise continued. Several minutes went by before she was awake and alert enough to realize that someone was beating on the front door.

Fear thudded in her heart as she flipped on a light and slid out of bed. Something must be dreadfully wrong, she thought dazedly. Nobody in his right mind would be knocking on someone's door at almost five A.M. A cold shudder of apprehension raced through her as she hurried into the living room.

Caution made her hesitate before opening the door. "Who is it?" she called. "What do you want?"

"Open the door, Jana! It's me, Miles!"

Miles! Complete shock paralyzed her while her

sleep-fuzzed mind tried to absorb it. Then, with fumbling fingers, she unbolted the door.

Miles stood there, framed by the doorway, looking worse than she had ever seen him. His sports shirt and slacks were crumpled, and his hair was disheveled. The dark shadow of a day's growth of beard appeared around his jaw and above his mouth. Deep hollows lurked beneath his bleary eyes.

Jana stared at him in horror. Unable to stop herself, she cried out, "What's wrong? What's wrong?" while her mind frantically worried that something dreadful had happened to someone in the family.

"You're what's wrong," Miles said in a grim, furious voice. Without being invited, he stepped past her into the room and kicked the door closed behind him. "God, Jana, what's wrong with you?"

She whitened, and confusion widened her eyes. "What are you talking about?" she asked breathlessly.

"How *could* you go away without telling me about our baby?" His dark eyes held bitter accusation.

"You know?"

"I know." The words fell heavily between them like stones dropping to the bottom of a pond.

"Holly," Jana murmured. "She told you after all."

Miles shook his head. "Guy told me."

"But he promised me!" Jana cried in outrage.

Miles smiled, but it was more of a sneer. "To give him credit, he didn't mean to tell me. It slipped out one night when he was bragging about becoming a father." He shook his head. "You wouldn't believe the change that's come over Guy and Edie. Lamaze classes, the whole bit. You'd think they were the first couple in the world to ever become parents."

The cozy vision that conjured up ripped into Jana's heart like a rusty saw. She turned away so she would no longer have to face Miles's hostile eyes.

"Guy didn't tell you where I am," she said suddenly, "because he didn't know."

"Allen Montgomery did that favor for me." In total astonishment, Jana swung around toward Miles and saw a grin lifting the corners of his mouth. "Actually, Holly was in on it, too. She called him and told him I was trying to find you. Between them, they correctly decided that I had a right to see you, so last night Allen called me." He raked a hand across his ashen face. "I went straight out to the car, and I've been driving all night." He leveled a long look at her. "Would it be too much to ask you to make me some coffee? Otherwise, I'm afraid I'll collapse right here where I'm standing."

"Of course," she answered stiffly. She turned toward the kitchen, unaware that he followed her and stood watching as she went through the mechanics of the simple chore.

"Nice apartment," Miles said casually from behind her.

She glanced around in surprise. "Yes."

"Small and cozy. Just right for a single person."

"Yes," she said again.

"That's why it won't do for you any longer."

Jana set the sugar bowl down onto the counter with a clatter. It tipped and spilled, but she hardly noticed. She was wary now, instinct telling her that Miles was setting some sort of trap and that she was the prey.

Two long strides carried him to her, and his arms slid around her waist, though he held her loosely so that they were standing face to face. "It'll be too crowded here for the three of us," he informed her.

His eyes, no longer accusing and hostile, now held a distinct twinkle.

"Three?" Jana echoed, feeling dull and stupid.

Miles nodded and bent to kiss the tip of her nose in a light, playful gesture. "You, me, and my daughter." One of his arms left its position around her and his hand gently patted the small swell of her midsection.

Jana was suddenly breathless, for there was a light burning in Miles's eyes that she had seen many times before, the light that had always been her undoing. Sternly, she glared at him. "It's my son," she said coldly, "and I don't remember your being invited to live here with us."

There was a dreamy quality to Miles's eyes, totally at odds with his usually sharp, keen gaze. "Twins," he decided. "A girl for me, a boy for you. So in that case we'll definitely need a larger place. A place like . . . hmm, how about the house we already have? That ought to hold us all, don't you think?"

Abruptly tired of Miles's teasing banter, Jana firmly removed his hands from around her and turned away. "I will not go back to you because of the baby, Miles."

"I'm not asking you to," he said quietly, and this time his voice was serious and thick, and he seemed to be having trouble speaking. "I'm not asking you to come back to me for our baby's sake, no matter how many advantages there might be just for that reason alone. I'm not asking you to make Mom a happy grandmother or Caroline a happy aunt, or to give Guy's and Edie's child a cousin for a playmate. I'm asking you to come back to me because I . . ." His voice became ragged. "I can't bear it without you."

Jana's shoulders were rigid with resistance when Miles's hands came down upon them and the warmth of his touch penetrated through the fabric of her robe. "Please come back to me," he said urgently. "Jana, I love you."

"You walked out on me this last time . . . remember?" she whispered over the tears in her throat.

"I was a fool!" Miles said heatedly. "My pride had been knocked cockeyed one more time, and I was hurt that you could still believe the worst about me. But, Jana, that night you said you loved me. Tell me now that you still do. You must!" His voice vibrated with intensity.

Slowly, she turned to gaze up into his strained, white face, and what she saw there melted her defenses. Her own fierce pride no longer seemed as important as it had yesterday.

"I love you, Miles," she said simply. "I always have. I always will."

A shuddering sigh rippled through Miles, and he drew her tenderly into his arms. His lips met hers, infinitely gentle and sweet at first, and then with a growing tide of passion. Her mouth parted beneath his in utter surrender, and his embrace tightened in fierce possession.

"I'll never let you go again," he told her huskily. They smiled into each other's eyes, a smile of understanding, of promise, and of infinite joy. "I'll make things up to you, precious heart, for the rest of our lives if you'll only forgive me for letting my stupid pride drive you away."

Jana shook her head, and the smile she gave him was soft and tender. "It's you who have the forgiving to do," she said unsteadily as her fingers ran lightly across the bristly stubble of his unshaven chin. "I'm sorry I lacked the faith and trust you deserved, Miles. But you were wrong to think that meant I didn't love you. I guess I just couldn't believe enough in myself to feel sure that nothing and no one could ever come between us."

A tiny smile parted Miles's lips. "Let's face it, precious heart, we've both been stupid, besides having far more pride than was good for us. Forgiveness and forgetfulness on both sides?"

Jana nodded. "Oh, yes, please." A spark of contentment lit her eyes like the sun peeping out from behind a rain cloud. "And when Miles, Jr. arrives, I intend to teach him early about the dangers of false pride . . . and jumping to conclusions."

Miles laughed, and a warm glow of color swept across his face, erasing the half-ill look of fatigue that had been there. "It'll be Jana, Jr., my darling, and I intend to tell her every day how much I love her and how very much I adore her mother. I hope," he said with a throaty catch to his voice, "that she looks just like you."

Jana gave a theatrical sigh. "I guess we *will* have to compromise and have twins. I'm determined it will be a son who's exactly like his father." Suddenly she giggled. "Can you imagine how much Parrish pride Dorothy will have if, in a few months, she had *three* grandchildren?"

Miles chuckled. "She'll be puffed up enough over two. We wouldn't be able to tolerate her if there were three. Maybe we'd better reconsider the twins. After all, we just decided too much pride is a dangerous thing."

"From now on," Jana decided in a firm voice, "the entire Parrish family is going to be proud *of* one another instead of using their pride against one another."

"Even of Edie?" he asked with an air of incredulity. "She used to cry in misery. Now she cries because she's happy. I don't know how Guy stands it! Next to marrying you, the luckiest thing that ever happened to me was when she broke our engagement and married my brother instead!"

Jana laughed, every shred of jealousy gone at last. "We're even going to be proud of her," she said firmly. "After all, she's about to make us an aunt and uncle." Now her eyes took on that same faraway, dreamy expression Miles's gaze had held earlier. "Can't you just see all our children playing together, ours and Guy's and someday Caroline's, too?"

"Hmm." Miles nuzzled her neck. "And Mom refereeing their squabbles while their parents go away on second, third, and fourth honeymoons."

"Then you don't think our love will grow dull and flat in time?" she teased as her fingers played sensuous little taps against his chest.

She was silenced with a kiss that shook her from head to toe. And the kiss itself was a vow between them, a bright and golden vow that ended all suffering and pain, a shiny, untarnished vow they would live up to for the rest of their lives.

6 brand new Silhouette Special Editions yours for 15 days–Free!

For the reader who wants more...more story...more detail and description...more realism...and more romance...in paperback originals, 1/3 longer than our regular Silhouette Romances. Love lingers longer in new Silhouette Special Editions. Love weaves an intricate, provocative path in a third more pages than you have just enjoyed. It is love as you have always wanted it to be—and more —intriguingly depicted by your favorite Silhouette authors in the inimitable Silhouette style.

15-Day Free Trial Offer

We will send you 6 new Silhouette Special Editions to keep for 15 days absolutely free! If you decide not to keep them, send them back to us, you pay nothing. But if you enjoy them as much as we think you will, keep them and pay the invoice enclosed with your trial shipment. You will then automatically become a member of the Special Edition Book Club and receive 6 more romances every month. There is no minimum number of books to buy and you can cancel at any time.

Silhouette Romance

IT'S YOUR OWN SPECIAL TIME

Contemporary romances for today's women.
Each month, six very special love stories will be yours
from SILHOUETTE. Look for them wherever books are sold
or order now from the coupon below.

$1.50 each

Hampson	☐ 1 ☐ 4 ☐ 16 ☐ 27 ☐ 28 ☐ 40 ☐ 52 ☐ 64 ☐ 94	Browning	☐ 12 ☐ 38 ☐ 53 ☐ 73 ☐ 93
Stanford	☐ 6 ☐ 25 ☐ 35 ☐ 46 ☐ 58 ☐ 88	Michaels	☐ 15 ☐ 32 ☐ 61 ☐ 87
		John	☐ 17 ☐ 34 ☐ 57 ☐ 85
Hastings	☐ 13 ☐ 26 ☐ 44 ☐ 67	Beckman	☐ 8 ☐ 37 ☐ 54 ☐ 72 ☐ 96
Vitek	☐ 33 ☐ 47 ☐ 66 ☐ 84		

$1.50 each

☐ 3 Powers	☐ 29 Wildman	☐ 56 Trent	☐ 79 Halldorson
☐ 5 Goforth	☐ 30 Dixon	☐ 59 Vernon	☐ 80 Stephens
☐ 7 Lewis	☐ 31 Halldorson	☐ 60 Hill	☐ 81 Roberts
☐ 9 Wilson	☐ 36 McKay	☐ 62 Hallston	☐ 82 Dailey
☐ 10 Caine	☐ 39 Sinclair	☐ 63 Brent	☐ 83 Hallston
☐ 11 Vernon	☐ 41 Owen	☐ 69 St. George	☐ 86 Adams
☐ 14 Oliver	☐ 42 Powers	☐ 70 Afton Bonds	☐ 89 James
☐ 19 Thornton	☐ 43 Robb	☐ 71 Ripy	☐ 90 Major
☐ 20 Fulford	☐ 45 Carroll	☐ 74 Trent	☐ 92 McKay
☐ 21 Richards	☐ 48 Wildman	☐ 75 Carroll	☐ 95 Wisdom
☐ 22 Stephens	☐ 49 Wisdom	☐ 76 Hardy	☐ 97 Clay
☐ 23 Edwards	☐ 50 Scott	☐ 77 Cork	☐ 98 St. George
☐ 24 Healy	☐ 55 Ladame	☐ 78 Oliver	☐ 99 Camp

$1.75 each

☐ 100 Stanford	☐ 105 Eden	☐ 110 Trent	☐ 115 John
☐ 101 Hardy	☐ 106 Dailey	☐ 111 South	☐ 116 Lindley
☐ 102 Hastings	☐ 107 Bright	☐ 112 Stanford	☐ 117 Scott
☐ 103 Cork	☐ 108 Hampson	☐ 113 Browning	☐ 118 Dailey
☐ 104 Vitek	☐ 109 Vernon	☐ 114 Michaels	☐ 119 Hampson

Silhouette ❤ *Romance*

15-Day Free Trial Offer
6 Silhouette Romances

6 Silhouette Romances, free for 15 days! We'll send you 6 new Silhouette Romances to keep for 15 days, absolutely free! If you decide not to keep them, send them back to us. You pay nothing.

Free Home Delivery. But if you enjoy them as much as we think you will, keep them by paying the invoice enclosed with your free trial shipment. We'll pay all shipping and handling charges. You get the convenience of Home Delivery and we pay the postage and handling charge each month.

Don't miss a copy. The Silhouette Book Club is the way to make sure you'll be able to receive every new romance we publish before they're sold out. There is no minimum number of books to buy and you can cancel at any time.

This offer expires July 31, 1982

Silhouette Book Club, Dept. SBL 17B
120 Brighton Road, Clifton, NJ 07012

    Please send me 6 Silhouette Romances to keep for 15 days,
    absolutely free. I understand I am not obligated to join the
    Silhouette Book Club unless I decide to keep them.

NAME_____

ADDRESS_____

CITY_____STATE_____ZIP_____